Alchemies of the Heart

DAVID DORIAN

Copyright © 2020 David Dorian
All rights reserved
First Edition

Fulton Books, Inc.
Meadville, PA

Published by Fulton Books 2020

ISBN 978-1-64654-494-3 (paperback)
ISBN 978-1-64654-495-0 (digital)

Printed in the United States of America

Inside the room at the psychiatrist's facility, by the window a luxuriant bush with opulent milk-white flowers scintillated under the morning rays.

Maren D'Arcy felt anesthetized as she walked into her husband's space where illness prevailed.

Gabriel D'Arcy sat placidly in the institutional armchair. His reverie had not been interrupted by his wife's intrusion.

She kissed him on the forehead, caressing the back of his neck. She sat on the bed and opened the paper bag. She opened the pastry box exposing a black forest cake.

"Happy birthday."

She unscrewed a bottle of a nonalcoholic prosecco and poured the pale liquid into two paper cups.

They sipped their drink in silence. She contemplated her husband, tracking a flicker of life across his eyelids, the whisper of breath in his throat.

His skin was wasting on his bones. His eyes had sunk a few inches deeper in his brows surrounded by patches of chalky skin. She had tried many times to enter his inner world, but to no avail. Impenetrable, he had remained asunder, sealed, out of range. That synchronicity they experienced in their married life had ended. What remained was an emotional tundra, inhospitable and uninhabitable. He had become a pale ghoul marooned among the living. Maren knew he was on the brink of the void.

"What're you reading?" she asked, picking up a book on his lap.

The Botany of Desire, she read out loud. The author asked, do plants use humans as much as we use them?

"Read it," he whispered with a muffled voice like a diver under water. Maren felt a wave of hope. He spoke to her.

She put the book in her bag. Maren brought a spoonful of cake to his mouth. Maybe he will taste the velvety chocolate, the frothy cream. Suddenly he squinted. A sliver of morning sun hurt his eyes. Maren muffled the sun with the curtain. She approached the flowery bush. A maroon spider hanging by a thread from a creamy-white dangling flower was weaving an elaborate web.

"I miss you," he muttered.

Maren was surprised.

The student nurse came by with a plastic cup containing multicolored pills.

Gabriel stood up and lurched toward the flowerpot. He inserted his hand inside the dirt and produced a black object. He limped toward his wife and handed it to her.

She stared at the USB flash drive and put it in her pocket.

Time leaked, unmeasured. They had been together for a few fragile moments, and she was pained by that sense of estrangement. The urge to leave was pressing. She kissed his forehead.

The visit had unleashed her stomach acids. A cruel heartburn was singeing her esophagus. There was so much unknown that had crashed into her life. Although arrived with shocking suddenness that horror devoured its prey. For days, it spreads its murkiness into every corner of her being. As hope had drained, a heavy weakness had descended on Maren. She suffered from complicated grief. Every day she lived her hours in an uncertain compromise with despair.

Gabriel had requested all the medical files of his condition to be off-limits to family and relatives. It was his prerogative. That action alienated her. Intrigued by her husband's secrecy, Maren lived in limbo. She was excluded from the treatment. Her amateurish interpretation of his symptoms led to a diagnosis of psychosis. The psychiatrists at the hospital hadn't helped. They confirmed a breakdown with reality, but they didn't explain why. They waited to be let in his inner sanctum. They medicated him, pacifying his inner turmoil. There were powerful antipsychotic drugs to counter that disease, and

Gabriel was put on three different medications. The chemical compounds he ingested kept him human.

Since Gabriel's hospitalization, Maren had immersed herself in her work expanding her yoga practice. The work distracted her. It engendered a welcomed stillness.

As she walked toward her Rover in the parking lot, that flash drive ensconced in the palm of her hand, she wondered what shattering secrets that device stored. Was it a portal or a breach into another world, the realm her husband inhabited?

Driving toward Manhattan, Maren was holding the electronic gadget tightly in her hand. Was it a key to some forbidden knowledge, to hell? Would she open that gate now and venture inside that dark domain, or delay? She wanted to throw that widget in the expressway. Her life would continue in that permanent state of not knowing, that purgatory of exalted ignorance. To decode the cryptogram concealed in the drive could modify her life, maybe forever. She entered the village of Little Neck. She parked her car outside a CVS pharmacy and went inside the store. She gulped four anti-acid tablets. On the same block, she located an internet café. She ordered a Moroccan mint tea and installed herself inside a booth. She slipped her debit card inside the slot then inserted the flash drive.

Her husband's words would appear on the monitor. Would they echo in her heart for the next hours, days, maybe eternity? She felt she was at the entrance of a labyrinth or at the edge of an abyss. A ringing of bells from the nearest church echoed. Was it an alarm alerting her she was stepping into forbidden grounds or a toll heralding the passing away of innocence?

She pressed Enter.

The Alchemy of the Heart

Alchemy: from Arabic "al-kimiya," the art and science of transmuting metals, also the quest for the universal solvent, the quintessence.

This document recorded in a USB drive is a biographical essay. It is commentaries on a kind of strife, a journal of upheavals in my last five years. It is an expedition into the province of my private lives. As you read it, you'll become my aide-de-camp, my confidant, my secretary. Don't judge me harshly. Like Freud said, sometimes we have to bend, even break some rules to maintain our humanity.

You'll ask, why am I writing these chronicles of events? Alvard Norst, my friend, wrote a personal journal documenting his disease, a skin condition that challenged every medical treatment available. He envisioned an account of his emotions as he battled his chronic illness. It was a rendition of his spiritual journey through the path of his ailment. Inspired by his endeavor, I decided to venture into biography, my own diary.

The written word conquers time. It survives erosion and oblivion and reemerges triumphant. To record time is a way of freezing time. Unlike photography, the written word is imperishable. But on the orders of Caliph Omar Ibn Al Khattab, the seven hundred thousand papyrus books of the library of Alexandria were burned at the cauldrons of the furnaces that heated water in the public baths.

To sharpen my writing style, I registered for online writing classes offered by the English Department at the New School. I applied myself to weekly writing assignments. My online professor identified in my writing a descriptive talent. She complimented my originality and praised the vibrancy of my imagery. My prose was a dormant medium that laid stagnant and would have lingered inert in my unconscious hadn't it been for my project to pen my memoirs. I expressed my gratitude for her encouragement and support and invited her to Balthazar, a French restaurant renowned for his Gascon chef. She turned me down because French cuisine didn't suit her culinary regimen. That's what she said. I've never been turned down by a woman before. I justified her rejection by convincing myself she had some food anxiety. She was very slim and slender, as a matter of fact. Was she anorectic? I was inconsolable for a while. My ego was bruised.

Shards of Glass

I'm prone to a pulmonary illness. My airways become easily inflamed. Extra mucus is produced inside the bronchi, which hinders respiration. Airborne agents trigger the lining of the bronchi. Acute asthma attacks require emergency response. Symptoms are alleviated with the inhalation of pharmaceutical chemicals which open the bronchi. Thanks to these devices, I can perform my duties, which require focused attention and vigilance. Inhalers save lives but do not heal. There is no cure provided by Western medicine.

All my life had been a single relentless attempt to flee an unremitting malaise: suffocation. For many years, I had to submit to the whims and commands of an uncertain health. It is impossible to enter a dialogue with a physical illness. There is blindness and obstinacy to pain. I had to endure its monologue, sustain its cruelty, submit to its tyranny, and with the support of analgesics, survive its assault on my humanity. It was a losing war interrupted from time to time by a precarious truce.

But the cough persisted in spite of medications and treatments from pulmonologists. Something alien and evil was blocking the airways, and the cough was an attempt to dislodge that irritant. Each sickness sends us a summons disguised as a question.

There is a psychogenic theory I find inspirational. It postulates a return to the airless conditions of the womb where oxygen is provided to the embryo through the mother's blood, not through the lungs. In the months of gestation, the lungs are undeveloped and primitive. Breathlessness is associated, therefore, with prenatal existence. It reestablishes that fusion with the mother. The human fetal larva is a sea creature. Is asthma a nostalgic longing for that amphibian aquatic state? During a flare-up, I literally drown in my own pulmonary mucus. It is a submersion in the liquid realm of bodily fluids and secretions. Back to the amniotic sea, therefore. Is it a latent wish to return to the mineral brine inside my mother's womb? It is a hypothesis of great mystical beauty. My imagination allows me to adorn and embellish reality.

I fabricate theories and axioms to entertain myself. It gives a colorful meaning to the enigmatic chemistry that rules our life.

The Vault of Memory

It's wrong to think that events stored in the vault of memory are preserved for all time, only to be uncovered by the ardent seeker. Many reminiscences, the majority of them are deleted. There are no traces of them as if the episodes they illustrated never happened.

How can we account for such acts of vandalism in the inner archives of the self? The only way to explain such massive destruction of accumulated data is to blame the neurochemical storms that play havoc in the meteorology of the brain. Memories are chemical structures subject to molecular upheavals. In this alchemy, change is inherent. That's why writing a diary is an endeavor to preserve events, to crystallize them into sentences and paragraphs, and by exposing them to others, they can live in other minds and survive the passage of time.

Panacea

Alvard shanghaied me for a drink one night at *Bar Lamia*. It was Alvard's favorite joint because of the variety of single malts they offered. Many patrons were fashion models, Wall Street executives, media people. Alvard never approached women at the bar. He didn't look for romance. He reminds me that the two greatest philosophers of love, Nietzsche and Schopenhauer, never loved a woman, preferring relationships with prostitutes. Alvard preferred brief liaisons with women of the night.

He was talkative that night at the bar. His mood was up.

"You know, my skin condition. I finally found the right treatment. She's Chinese, did her medical studies at Beijing University. I'm telling you, she has manna in her hands," he claimed.

He paused and took a sip of Bowmore.

"You should try her," he said.

"Is she your new belle-de-nuit?"

"Oh no, she's strictly massage."

"You're feeling better?"

"Never felt better. She must be a reincarnation of Bien Que."

"Who is he?"

"The first doctor in Chinese medical history. They called him 'the doctor who brings back his patients from the dead.'"

"Sounds like voodoo."

"I don't give a damn! As long as it works."

"Doesn't sound very scientific," I said.

"Give her a try, for your asthma. You will be in good hands. Excuse the word play. Just pay her a visit. Just imagine a future without your inhalers," he said.

The Confessions of Wounds

Although a journal is mostly for private consumption, it will fall predictably into other hands. Behind the mask of privacy lurks an exhibitionist. Because the log is a depository of secrets, there is a good chance they'll be divulged. A secretary was originally a piece of furniture made of wood, a writing desk with locked drawers designed to shelter the private correspondence of government officials or the intimate letters of aristocratic women. The confidante who managed such a precious piece of furniture, the keeper of the keys to drawers, was called a *secretaire*, the guardian of the secrets. But as etymology reveals, the word *secret* derives from the Latin word *secretus*, meaning "separate, hidden," and the French word *secreter*, which has given the English words "to secrete" and "secretion," means "to discharge, to seep, to excrete what is hidden." Thus, a secret is meant to be discharged, released. There's an uncanny paradox embedded in that word. Every diary is a prolonged confession to be leaked.

The Art of Breathing

There is another interpretation of my malady. To breathe is to allow the outside in, to accept the intrusion of reality, to condone the invasion of our body. We breathe when we enter this world. We speak of our first breath and our last breath. Cioran said, "*Only the idiot is equipped to breathe.*" Based on this cynical remark, I dare say, "The real gives me asthma."

But I think the real disease is life itself. Is my diary an analysis of an illness camouflaged behind a pulmonary condition?

When Crustaceans Love

I drove to the address on Fifth Avenue. I walked for a while on the wide pavement, examining Armani windows. That evening air had an odor of burned plastic and sweat. My breathing was labored. I had my inhaler in my jacket pocket just in case. I stopped at *Le Pain Quotidien* on Broadway and ordered a coffee with a *petit pain au chocolat*. I sat down on the long communal table and sipped my brew. An elderly man, dressed fashionably, was sending an e-mail to someone called Sebastian. That's a name one doesn't hear anymore since *Suddenly Last Summer*, that play by Tennessee Williams which was turned into a movie with Montgomery Cliff and Elizabeth Taylor. My oblique gaze read: "*It was going to end anyway, and you knew it, there's no solution.*" He was breaking up with his beau. Was it a suicide note? Should I engage in a therapeutic dialogue, flash my medical credentials, and save his tortured life? He beckoned the waiter and ordered a tarte aux framboises. French pastry saved the day.

I rang the ninth floor. The elevator ascended, straining and whining. On the landing, there were three doors like in fairy tales. On one door, a Chinese word was painted in red in a flamboyant calligraphy.

The bell sounded like chimes caressed by a sea breeze. An old Chinese lady ushered me into the massage room. I asked her about the word painted on the wall in the landing.

"Ah, yes. Tiantang. That is 'heaven' in Mandarin," she echoed.

The wilted card on the pale-yellow wall read:

> *This is a legitimate establishment. Do not ask the attendant to perform any act of a sexual nature.*

DAVID DORIAN

*If you do, it will be denied and you will
not have access to these premises.
Thank you for your understanding
and your cooperation.*
—The Management

Then, why the dimmer, that plastic knob in the wall, which, with a flip from the finger, could regulate the luminosity of an incandescent bulb, turning it into a thousand suns or instill the darkness of interstellar space where the apotheosis would be consummated?

A Chinese screen flashed a Buddha with androgynous lips gleaming with the lure of a promised nirvana. His pale hand was holding a flowering bush of droopy, trumpetlike white flowers.

I took off my jacket, unbuttoned my shirt, and donned a sandalwood-scented kimono. It was a pastel-green robe with embroidered cranes engaged in a mating dance.

I stretched my body on the massage table.

On a wall, I noticed a print of a painting of Hokusai's *Dream of the Fisherman's Wife*. In this canvas, a reclining geisha is being orally assaulted by an octopus. I was transfixed by the woman ravished by a mollusk, the ravenous beak of the crustacean digging into her fleshy corolla. The image was intriguing for a legitimate massage establishment.

The door gyrated, and a shadow filtered in. She looked thirty, but I knew her face sealed a secret of the mystery of aging. Asian women weather artfully the ravages of time. Their ivory faces and nubile alabaster skin are impervious to the erosion of aging. There is a timelessness about their physique and an eternity about their physiognomy. An elegance of lines, an eggshell skin coloring graced her ovoid face. Utamaro would have committed seppuku to have her as a model in his depiction of the women of *The Floating World*.

She removed my kimono. I pointed with my fingers at my bronchi where the disease was lodged. An enchanting melody from *Madame Butterfly* filled the room.

Examining the contours of her well-penciled eyes, I traveled in time. I recalled photographs of movie actresses from the fifties—

Garbo, Stanwick, Blyth, etc.—whose dreamy gazes turned inward. Everything about those women spelled the sublime.

Light dimmed to its ultimate blackness.

I was blind like a one-celled organism in the primordial sea, tethered to the world by her precarious touch, connected to the living by a cutaneous anchor. I complied, surrendering my body to her inquisitive hands, capitulating to her lubricating touch.

Ointments basted my body. Oiled hands kneaded dormant muscles in silence.

Time streamed beyond consciousness or reason.

Voices chanting a Buddhist sutra rose rapidly to a crescendo. I was inside a monastery with monks intoning sacred words in Pali. The incantation magnified my inward emptiness. Filled with the void, I witnessed the annihilation of my self. Memory evaporated in the vacant universe.

I got dressed, sluggishly. The air I was inhaling was ethereal. Objects had lost their angularity.

I left money on the massage table. I don't know how much.

"I am Gabriel, and you?" I muttered as I limped toward the door.

"Mantuo Luo."

I ventured into the street feeling diaphanous and vaporous like an inebriated monarch butterfly in the beginning of its migration to Mexico. The day poured out, and with it departed the man I used to be. That unforgettable afternoon, I had received my stigmata.

Words of Annihilation

To acquaint myself with writing a diary, I studied literary examples: *The Confessions* of Saint Augustine, *The Confessions of an English Opium Eater* by Thomas DeQuincey, *Confessions* of Jean-Jacque Rousseau. Many autobiographies are confessions. I read also Dostoyevsky's *Notes from the Underground,* Nabokov's *Lolita, Confession of a Dutiful Daughter* by Simone de Beauvoir, *Nausea* by Jean-Paul Sartre. I explored erotic confessions: I read Casanova's autobiography and Catherine Millet's memoir, *The Sexual Life of Catherine M., The Surrender* by Toni Bentley.

A Return to Hades

Three days later, I visited her again. The chest congestion had subsided during the following week. The shards of glass that perforated my alveoli had lost their keenness.

The holidays were upon us. My wife and I became swept in the orgy of shopping that marks the weeks that preceded Christmas, yet in spite of the running around, I didn't cough.

The holiday anxiety was taking its toll on my wife. The visit of her family, the arrival of her father complicated the stress. The travel logistics of all the members were an ordeal I endured this time around without duress. My wife was an Episcopalian, and the holidays were an opportunity to summon all the usual family suspects from all the corners of the empire for a series of lavish dinners, which she executed out of duty instead of adherence to a faith she had abandoned years ago.

Images of Mantuo Luo illuminated me from the inside. Knowing I would visit her soon made the stressful season more tolerable. It was her gaze—aloof, remote, fully detached, yet engaging—that had pierced me. I had been stunned, subjugated, disarmed by the stare. In that last encounter, her cool, imperious gaze had seeded my memory. It had germinated sprouting branches in the soil of the self.

Echoes of Distant Bells

A diary! It's the motivation of memorialists to expose themselves and seek absolution. They don't know what they should be redeemed from. They can't escape a perpetual malaise at the core of their being. After Freud, journal writers became engaged in self-analysis emboldened by a new arsenal. They excavated the strata of the self in quest of repressed trauma.

In this present autobiography of the last three years of my life, I won't ignore distasteful details or enshrine triumphs. I'll flagrantly divulge my sins. Confessions lead to torture chambers. Every journal writer is a mini Freud; every diary keeper, a lay analyst. Freud practiced self-analysis throughout his life, self-examining his emotions, unconscious thoughts, latent desires. My discovery of this mentalist was a hand grenade thrown at the fortress of my self. I delved into his writings with the sacred curiosity and saintly eagerness of a pilgrim on the road to Damascus.

*****

My wife was appreciating my good spirit which had replaced my intermittent cynicism. This anonymous Asian woman I had visited a few times was altering my mood by soothing my pulmonary discomfort and alleviating my innate discontent.

An inner revolution had started. This Oriental agent provocateur threw a Molotov cocktail on my ramparts. She helped me overthrow myself.

*****

My wife traveled to Washington, DC, to help decorate her sister's apartment.

I drove to the city. The air on Fifth Avenue reeked of car exhaust fumes and women's perfume.

The elevator groaned as it struggled to the ninth floor. The elderly Chinese lady ushered me in. She took my hand and squeezed it.

I undressed and lay down in the massage table.

Her moist fingers unleashed a torrent cascading down my chest, loosening gnarled muscles, pulverizing recalcitrant nerves, unearthing obstructing rocks, uprooting petrified roots. The stream of effervescent feelings turned into a river rushing toward a waterfall. My body, now liquefied, fell into the abyss of the white rapids. A sudden serenity permeated every molecule of my epidermis. I was nudged by a gentle current like a sailboat caressed by temperate winds. The benevolent tide escorted me to a large estuary, and the drift deposited me on a protruding coral bank covered with soft aquamarine grass.

I left that massage session with a stillness and emptiness. My chest kept improving, getting stronger after each encounter with my nurse. Everyone has had, at any given moment, an extraordinary experience which will be for him, because of the memory of it he preserves, the crucial stimulus to his inner modification. Memories of college poetry courses I had taken during a summer session at Columbia University emerged. Poetic lines read by an inspired teacher trickled. The words from the Persian poet Al Ghazali echoed:

> *Are you ready to cut off your head and place your foot on it? The cost of the elixir of love is your head. Do you hesitate?*

*****

This journal would start a dialogue with myself and build new relationships with other parts of my soul. This salvage operation within myself could retrieve sunken ships. It's through conversations that truths are revealed. Suspects are exposed while chatting. Writing could be a start of a new liaison with myself. It's still better than slashing my wrists with a rusted razor.

Anchors in the Past

Returning home after a visit with Mantuo Luo, I turned on the car radio. The male voice sounded intelligent and authoritative. He was a Hindu guru named Moksha, which means "release."

Every time we dwell on the past, every time we return to a painful episode, we increase the possibility of reproducing it. Every time we remember a past trauma, we reinforce the neurocircuit; we rearm it. Instead of progressing, we are regressing. That is the problem with psychoanalysis, the product of a Jewish mind accustomed to be mistreated and persecuted. Freud was the inheritor of five thousand years of trauma. His father endured anti-Semitic remarks in the street of Vienna. He faced academic criticism for his theories of infantile sexuality. Disappointments, sadness, bad memories anchor us in the past. To bypass the past, we should avoid talking about it at all costs, burn photos, get rid of all objects that are associated with painful experiences. We should welcome amnesia. Bad memories, if not revived, disintegrate. The circuit is disarmed.

I was intrigued by his views on mental health. All therapeutic endeavors aim at exhuming the past to neutralize its toxicity. Could all these psychologists be wrong? We believe our memories define us. I am what I have experienced and done. Identity is biography, and biography is psychology. Everyone believes it is so. Our traumas explain us; our remembrances determine us.

If this approach, which is to keep on emerging the traumas, is erroneous and we could find ways to circumvent the traumas without dwelling on them, it would put a lot of mental health professionals out of a job. But without trauma, world literature wouldn't exist. Literature and art are attempts to deal with trauma. Trauma is responsible for human civilization.

There was a commercial on the radio. An American company was promoting a special brush specifically designed for dogs when they are shedding. It offered 79 percent more hair absorption than the standard hairbrush for dogs. Users of this product were interviewed and expressed in enthusiastic language how that brush literally saved their lives by making the air cleaner in their home.

The interview continued. Moksha recommended to consciously and deliberately block those memories. Do not let your mind visit that emotional injury in your past. Do not linger around events that had become agonizing souvenirs. Forgetting is divine. We are all innate masochists, he claimed, attracted by all forms of suffering. That is a derangement that is common to us all.

Our torment is of our own making. Isn't enough that we have been hurt by these happenings? Why do we revisit them again and again? Why do we replay those scenes ad nauseam, savoring the hardships we had encountered at some points in our infancy, childhood, adolescence, and adulthood? We are haunted by what has been done to us. Not only we are victimized by what has happened to us, but we are doubly victimized by the memories of the bad things that happened to us. End the persecutions now. This is a self-inflicted martyrdom that has to stop, for our sake, so we can live completely in the present and relish our presence in the world of here and now.

The Whipping Post

Around 4:00 AM, the village of Rye, New York, looked like a deserted hamlet with its fossilized streets where time had petrified. The land where the hamlet of Rye was built was purchased from the Mohegan Indians by settlers from Long Island. There was nothing remarkable about that town. Perhaps the most revealing feature was the public post where, long time ago, slaves were bound to be whipped. It was located on the village green close to Christ's Church. Thomas Ricket was appointed as the town "public whipper." In 1682 it was a misdemeanor, punishable by flogging, for more than four slaves to meet together. It was reduced to three around 1730. I didn't know the secret history of that town when I bought my house. I was thinking of moving to another town when I found out that all the hamlets of Westchester County had their own "whipper."

An eerie breeze was blowing. The night air was glistening. It was scented by the abundant foliage, spiced by the luxuriant lilac bushes my wife had planted in the front yard. My breathing was effortless. I could feel my lungs expanding, sucking in that lush air.

Were there signs of the approaching atrocities, foreshadowings of future calamities? There was no cue, no premonition that the blooming garden of our lives would be decimated by the approaching storm. No hints the gods were offended. No seismograph of the soul would have registered the tremors that were to disassemble our felicitous existence. The lives of all the participants of this play were coming to an intersection, a crossroad that would disorient the most seasoned navigator. Yet how predestined it all seemed.

I was back in the solid geometry of our bedroom. In the massage spa, I had survived an arson to my ordered life, yet I had not pulverized the idols of the hearth. The world didn't cave in. My cat,

Miou, greeted me with a languorous yawn. I slipped under the covers and curled into bed. Eons came and went while I hovered over the suburbs of sleep. I couldn't fade into that blessed state of unconsciousness. I drifted like a kite tethered to reality only by the memory of her. My joy spiraled into rapture at the anticipation of the next encounter.

The first rays of Sunday molested the sheer curtains, ravished the bedsheets, exposing my fading dissolution. Reality's hold was de rigueur once again. I drowned in the immense solitude of that compulsively ordered room. My chest reverberated from echoes of a distant bell.

I wondered, lying in the unbearable softness of the comforter, slashed by stalactites of guilt whether I could find a sanctuary in my house. The train of thought, once having left the station, became a runaway locomotive. The room responded with soft sighs of anticipation. Sedition simmered in my heart.

Things I thought as absolute were changing. From a particular optic, nothing shattering had occurred except my unbearable presence in the world. The body I was occupying, although healing physically, was morally less than its former glory. I was a monster hybrid suddenly grafted to an unknown stem. Unrecognized sap flowed in me. What blossoms would bloom from such a graft?

I walked down the stairs to the basement where my wife had installed a mini-gym. I turned on my Samsung 65 Class Slim Curved 4K Ultra HD LED Smart TV with built-in WiFi and mounted my Schwinn AD6 Airdyne cycling machine. The TV spokesperson was commenting about the new dating trends. Dating websites were attracting college students, housewives, and women in middle management. College students in need of cash were flashing photoshopped photographs of their bodies offering companionships for men for a gratuity. The cost of tuition, books, living accommodations was enormous. Financially stressed undergraduate coeds found a pragmatic solution to their economic distress. Girls from Ivy League colleges were interviewed by reporters. Many housewives registered to those websites anonymously, photographs on request. Dulled by the routine nature of their married lives, they spiced up their afternoons with a little dalliance with men dulled by the routine nature of their married lives. Like in Bunuel's *Belle de Jour*, they performed sex in the afternoon for a negotiable fee. The narrator addressed the prevalence of single professional women in banking, law, teaching, advertising, insurance, etc. who indulged in special arrangements. They'd didn't want a "serious relationship," preferring to hook up with appropriate strangers. The menu du jour was polygyny and polyandry. The analyst then reported the new popularity of polyamory clubs, sex clubs, wife swapping, etc.

    My legs were hurting like crazy from the strenuous artificial biking. I fell asleep on the faux-leather couch. Time passed unrecorded. When I woke up, my cervical vertebrae were hurting a lot. The television was still on, featuring a documentary, *When Fish Attack*, showing many assaults on preys by sharks, barracudas, swordfish, eels, rays, sea snakes, etc.

Two Time Zones

I showered and got dressed. I walked back to the bedroom to retrieve my watch on the night table. It ran thirty-six minutes ahead. It marked an unlived future. This Swiss watch didn't depend on a battery. It picked up the vibrations of the hand movements which oscillates a tuning fork. It had been, till now, an accurate chronometer offered for my fortieth birthday by my wife. I pressed it to my ear. Mechanical arrhythmia was the diagnosis. It was still measuring time, but not the time I was living in. I stored it in my pocket, promising to visit a watchmaker. This Swiss watch had been crafted with aplomb by artisans who had taken precision to a standard of the highest order. Was this time monitor responding to a schism in my time continuum? Was its delicate and sensitive mechanism, the indented wheels and gears designed and cut by artful craftsmen, compromised? Had the pinions and sprockets been affected by my emotional crisis precipitated by my existence in two chronological time zones?

Our heart is a time machine, like a chronometer in music. It measures the passage of that dimension and establishes a cadence. We are all allotted a certain number of beats. And then the mechanism ceases. We call it cardiac arrest. The watch was strapped to my wrist and was picking up heartbeats and the rhythm of blood gushing through my arteries. The pulse of a subject is taken by pressing that articulation point of the metacarpus. My watch sensed my pulse on a continuous basis. It oscillated the tuning fork. Was it now reacting to my asymmetrical heartbeat? Was the beat of my watch altered by an intermittent heart?

*****

Alvard had invited me to *Delilah*'s, a soul food restaurant bar on First Avenue. I ordered a bourbon, and he asked for Perrier.

"She's gifted, your masseuse," I voiced.

"In the twelfth century she'd burn at the stake," he said.

"You think she's a witch?" I intoned.

"Who cares?"

"I've been reading about massage. They talk of a spiritual transcendence achieved by some patients during massage sessions. I don't know. Maybe that's what I felt after she finished with me. How did you find her?" I asked.

"I was doing a gig at *Jezebel*'s in Harlem. I was buddy with the owner Hadrian Vergilius, a guy from Martinique. He had a side business. He'd deliver girls to chic pubs and bars uptown. Pimp extraordinaire. I became the physician for all the girls. Maintained hygiene, you know. Hadrian's drinking was getting worse. He tried AA. The booze was killing him. One night I drove him to an AA meeting, and there she was. He met her there. She was networking for her business. Plenty of potential customers there. He scheduled an appointment. After three massage sessions, he couldn't touch alcohol."

AA is a circle of Dante's hell, a sanctuary for the damned, a holding cell. Lost souls congregated in those rooms seeking rescue and salvation, Alvard explained. Her beauty was a lure for down-and-out men whose egos were diminished by their debilitating addictions. They thought they could munch on her Asian pussy. They all became her patients. She haunted that subterranean underworld inhabited by sinners, offering glimmers of hope to helpless souls. The resurrection she peddled was accessible. She would touch their ailing skin, caress their neglected epidermis. And they wouldn't drink anymore.

"And she doesn't even speak English," Alvard said.

He sipped his Perrier.

"She talks with her hands. She's a Walkyrie," he said.

"What're you talking about?"

"A Walkyrie, a Chooser of the Dead. She picks wounded warriors in the battlefield and flies them to Valhalla," he said.

"He's still her client?" I asked.

"Who?"

"Hadrian."

"Died in a car crash."

"What happened?"

"Hadrian bought a beach bungalow in Ogunquit, Maine. A foreclosure deal. Very cheap. We'd hang out there, in the summer, and eat lobsters 24-7. The police report said it was highway fatigue. He'd been driving for eleven hours. He was sober when he had the accident."

The Yanks Are Coming

We all worry to death about the circumstances of our death. It is our birth that should preoccupy us. Today is my birthday.

Forty-nine years ago, a stray shell from a twelve-inch naval gun from an American Destroyer stationed five miles from the North African Coast hit the short-stay Hotel Sevigny at Rue Lasalle and tore it to shreds. The thunder created by the nearby explosion stunned my mother. I came out of her womb ejected into the sound and the fury of Operation Torch, the American landing in Casablanca, Morocco.

"Quel jour pour naitre," Mother moaned.

"I va etre en colere toute sa vie parce qu'il est ne pendant un bombardement," Solange, the neighbor, commented.

My mother sent Solange to fetch the priest so I'd be baptized, in case I'd die that day. By that rite, she would secure my entrance into the next world. Solange returned empty-handed. The church had been hit by an American shell and had caved in, and the priest had given up the ghost under a mountain of beams from the collapsed roof. I was never baptized.

Dense smoke from the burning hotel choked the neighboring streets. The singed walls smoldered for days. I inhaled these exhalations, which incinerated my throat and filled my eyes with tears. Is that what caused my asthma?

After the fall of France, my father took a bus to Tangiers, crossed the straits of Gibraltar on a fishing boat, hitchhiked through Spain, and crossed the Pyrenees to Provence, where he joined the partisans. He filled the ranks of the Resistance, which attracted students and French Army deserters who refused to collaborate with the invaders. He had become a combatant, placing explosives on railroad tracks, derailing troupe transports, slaughtering garrisons. He didn't know he had a son. I never knew I had a father.

My mother, who made a living from tips as a waitress in the *bistrot* Café du Soleil, a dive for a garden variety of local alcoholics and American infantrymen, found herself without employment as the eating establishment was looted by starving Arabs. Desperate to feed me and trapped for cash, she opened her apartment to American soldiers garrisoned in the city, turning her two rooms into a bed-and-breakfast for the victors. The guests didn't come empty-handed. Their ticket to my mother's cuisine and her bed were canisters of evaporated milk and large boxes of salted butter. I owe my strong bones to the rivers of American milk and Wisconsin butter I devoured.

My mother was an alluring woman: alabaster skin, maroon eyes, cascading hazel-colored hair. A Captain Jim Martin, from New York, was a repeat visitor. He played the banjo and laughed for no reason. He would bring chocolate, a luxury item in a time of famine, from the military PX. Jim was a superb American: jovial and generous. He married my mother before he went to kill more Germans. His unit moved across North Africa, stalking the retreating Afrika Corp. He escorted General Patton across Sicily, Italy, and the Ardennes. He returned triumphant, many dollars in his pockets. To the victor belongs the spoils. He hauled Mother and me to the New World. We moved to Jackson Heights, Queens, New York, into a two-bedroom apartment with a balcony full of pots where my mother cultivated *fines herbes*.

I have to thank the States of Wisconsin and Michigan for my survival. Before the Americans landed, kids in North Africa were dying of starvation. The French had requisitioned the crops for the German army fighting the Russians, leaving nothing for the local population. The GIs entered the city and with truckloads of powdered milk in tow. Thousands of babies—French, Jews, and Arabs born in the war years—are alive today because of the Yankees.

I never met my biological father. I was told he was arrested by the Gestapo in Dijon with his Resistance friends and executed. This information arrived in a letter addressed to my mother by the Bureau of Disappeared Persons organized by the new French government. My mother told me I looked like him.

Teen Angel

If I had caressed Marge DiAngelo's breasts that evening, my life would have been altered forever. While waiting in line outside the Forest Hills movie theater featuring shorts of Charlie Chaplin, she had deliberately struck up a conversation. During the film, she had put her arm on the armrest. The imagined scent of her nipples preoccupied me more than the spastic gestures of that English comic. *Hold her hand!* I kept saying to myself. It was a defining moment, trivial, distorted, grotesque. The afternoon ended in a terrible emptiness. It could be summed up in a single word: *dread*.

At the age of fifteen, progesterone and estrogen, secreted by the ovaries, produce pads of fatty tissue around the breast and buttocks. Samantha Waters's face was exceptional. When I saw her the first time making an entrance in my chemistry class in the hallway, I felt violent contractions in my lower abdomen. Sexual frustration manifests itself as intense tightening of the abdominal area as sperm backs up.

At the age of fifteen, she had not noticed that silence reigned when she entered in a public place: classroom, café, bookstore, library. Like everyone else, I revered her, from a distance. Idolatry is a religion. Teenagers are pagans. They've not been converted yet to the cult of compassion. Because of her beauty, she was deemed unapproachable. Everybody felt she was out of their league. Good guys didn't have the guts to ask her out. They couldn't imagine they could ever get near her breasts. The low-life elements in school hit on her.

Great beauty seems invariably to foreshadow some tragic fate. She lost her virginity to a meth addict who wasn't intimidated by her unearthly beauty. I couldn't explain why Dante's Beatrice would suck a gnome's cock? Didn't Venus marry that ugly god of war, Mars?

As a future medical student curious about the behavior of organs, I learned that the shaft of the clitoris is covered by Krause's corpuscles rich in nerve endings. When touched, they send signals to the brain which releases endorphins.

It isn't the first time a classy woman fell for a simian. There's nothing more archaic and pathetic than a teenage boy with a perennial hard-on. I've read in some book on the psychopathology of seduction that ancillary affairs have an erotic component. It's the eternal theme of the beauty and the beast.

Samantha Waters's association with Antonio Lope de Vega spelled doom for this angel of light. It was a first step in an irrevocable decline. Her boyfriend sent her on errands to his clients. She was bartered for drugs. And then one day, she stopped coming to school. The principal told the kids in the assembly hall that she had vanished. Agents came to interrogate her friends in school.

I remember, after the disappearance of Samantha, I became addicted to serial-killers novels and movies. The perpetrators were all psychotic, autistic, mentally deranged boys who couldn't get laid. I studied the high school and college homicidal maniacs who went on a rampage on campuses all over the country. I collected and cataloged mountains of data. What became apparent and was lost on all the state forensic psychologists, reporters, journalists, radio and TV commentators was that those kids were horny adolescents who couldn't get laid. The sexual frustration was so piercing, the orgastic blockage so oppressive that they detonated in the only way they could, through a different kind of sublimated discharge. They disburdened themselves, unloaded their repressed lust through the barrels of handguns. They experienced the euphoria and hysteria, the spasms, their body racked by the coital recoil of a fired Glock.

The Scented Octopus

My hours in college were under the gravitational pull of the goddess. The proximity of a woman's body plunged me into a state of agitation. I was a biology student at Queens College in Queens, New York. Girls from immigrant families filled classrooms. They were girls from Peru, Greece, Korea, Finland sitting on these narrow seats, their legs exposed, their sweaters stretched by blooming glands. I endured a constant erection. During the day, between classes, I'd rush into the men's room to relieve myself, giving some slack to the taut skin of my penis. I then stored my now-limp penis in my brief, belted my pants, and joined my fellow students in the lecture hall to hear my professor's discourse on molecular biology. I realized then an obvious truth, that genitals are a source of permanent, available, accessible pleasure. It was a compensation from all the ills the flesh is heir to. Genitals make us cling to life. And when other organs let us down one by one, as we endure the degeneration and humiliation of old age, we grip our sagging balls and rub our penises and feel that élan vital which makes life a vibrant journey.

The windowless auditorium was badly ventilated, and the feminine scents infused this closed planet. I was captivated by the feminine audience. I was calculating the mathematical probability of girls menstruating simultaneously in this place and time. The auditorium was full, all its five hundred seats occupied. I speculated 60 percent were women. They were at least around three hundred female students. I entertained there must have been at least seventy-five women having their period in the here and now, to use Eckhart Tolle's expression which sold him a lot of books turning a German hobbit into a rich ascetic. Many students were wearing skirts, which promoted the aeration of their vaginas. That vesicle, the feminine organ, is not a lifeless amalgam of cells. Secretions lubricate it and protect it from bacterial infections. It exudes aromas. Didn't the twelfth-century Tunisian Berber Umar Nafzawi write the erotic masterpiece *The Perfumed Garden* at the request of the sultan of Tunis Aziz Al Matawakki? I was inhaling a rich, scented air that didn't in any way trigger my asthma. I rejoiced at the fact that I wasn't allergic to women's odors.

Years passed. I forgot about Samantha. One evening, I was alone in the house. I defrosted salmon and was marinating it in an olive tapenade in preparation for frying. I poured myself a glass of Graves. The program *Cold Cases* was on. It was about crimes that hadn't been solved because the investigation had failed to identify any suspects and time had passed without any new piece of evidence. The reporter was examining the case of Samantha Waters. Photographs of the victim flashed on the screen. Interviews with friends and neighbors were replayed. There was nothing new in the investigation. Her parents made an appeal for anyone who had some information to call a particular number. Anonymity was promised. The sum of thirty thousand dollars was allocated to anyone with a solid lead.

Sleep evaded me that night. I swallowed three clonazepams.

I don't know why, after I had seen Samantha in that *Cold Cases* show, I bought a finch. I got a spacious cage with swings. But the bird was mute. It was autistic, I figured. I found out finches don't like to be alone. I got my zebra finch a companion. I placed it in the cage. The excitement was palpable as they flew around the cage performing a mating dance. A romance flourished. In a few days, music filled the room. They were both singing—sometimes solo, other times duos. I called it harmonic resonance.

Nerve Endings

When I came home around eight o'clock, the dining room table was well-appointed. Crystal goblets reflected the flames from elongated blue candles in silver holders. My wife uncorked the bottle of chilled Chenin Blanc.

"I've prepared canard à l'orange with a Grand Marnier sauce for your birthday. I didn't invite your friends as you requested."

"Thank you."

I hate birthdays, particularly my own. I am susceptible to amnesia around that time of the year. I'm always reminded of that day by family and friends.

I washed my hands stinking of acrid hospital antiseptic soap and sat close to my wife.

"Your mother called. She'd like you to visit her. She has a present for your birthday."

"I'll call her."

Maren disappeared in the kitchen. The house was quiet. I cherished the momentary stillness. A compulsive woodpecker perched on one of the tall trees around the house was banging its head against a resilient bark. Its hammering disturbed the delicate serenity of that bucolic evening. I had escaped the mechanical jackhammers manned by Honduran workers slaving for Con Edison in the city, tearing the asphalt on Lexington Avenue outside my office. I had sought refuge in an arboreal suburb. Now in this rustic milieu, this bipolar bird with its beak was pulverizing the exterior membrane of a tree in search for insects hiding inside the trunk. There are government environmental agencies that monitor noise levels. This incident became magnified, forgetting that my birthday neurosis goes into high gear around the day of my entry into this world. I gulped my wine hoping the alcohol would sedate my disgruntled.

"I've been thinking of turning our attic into a yoga studio," my wife dropped.

I was in no mood to discuss house renovation: workers traipsing on my floors with their industrial boots dragging planks of wood and sheetrock.

"You think it's a good idea?" she asked.

"I don't know," I groaned.

"I'd like to start teaching again. Maybe you'll take some classes."

"Why don't you rent studio space in some gym."

"I can do that, but I'd prefer having my own studio, and the attic is perfect."

"What about privacy? Students will be coming in and out. I don't want to turn my home into a school. It's a residence, not a dojo."

"The classes will be in the evening, and you're never here in the evening."

"And on weekends? Housewives flock to yoga classes on weekends."

"I won't do weekends."

"What's for dessert?"

"Black forest cake."

She walked to the kitchen and returned with a tray with a coffeepot and the cake.

"What kind of renovation?" I asked.

"I scheduled appointments with flooring contractors. I've not signed any contract. I wanted to talk to you first. I think some white pine flooring will gave the attic a pristine look."

"Pristine? You want to build a shrine?"

"No, just a place that's welcoming, a place for relaxation. We have to remove some boxes and store them in the garage," she said. "I found photos."

Maren handed me a cardboard box full of snapshots illustrating many stages of Captain Jim Martin's life: a smiling infant, an impish child, a clownish adolescent, a virile young man. An album contained grainy sepia snapshots of my stepfather in uniform with his army buddies. Many photographs highlighted an exuberant liberator of many Italian towns, surrounded by local Italian girls. In a photograph shot in an aristocratic living room belonging to some Junker, my father was sitting on a Baroque chair, throne-like, brandishing captured enemy flags, banners, and weapons he had looted from the retreating Germans.

"Your father had lots of fun in Europe," Maren commented.

"That's why men go to war," I said.

"There's no war for you, my love," she launched.

I didn't rise to the provocation.

Every dawn I enter the operating room, I engage the enemy. It's a carnage with many casualties. The clash lasts for hours. Sometimes, I am soundly beaten; other times, I prevail. Hostilities never end. There is a truce. We call it health. In those periods of nonaggression, life begins again, but not for long. The virus or the bacteria or some weak cellular tissue ruptures, or some accident rips organs, and the patients are rushed to the operating room, and I am summoned to plan the next assault.

I set the photo album aside and continued prospecting my black forest cake.

That night, my wife made love to me. Her body, I had thought, held no mysteries. I had caressed, tasted its fragrant sweetness a thousand times. Her geography, which I thought I knew intimately, now seemed alien. Her surfaces were alluringly unfamiliar. Her skin, which I had caressed countless times, was unidentifiable. Did my wife sense the proximity of another woman, a potential rival? Did that subliminal awareness cause glands to secrete more estrogen to oversexualize Maren, now threatened by Mantuo Luo? Estrogen, the female hormone is a Greek word—*oistros*, meaning literally "verve" and "inspiration" and the suffix "gen," which is "producer of." Estrogen is the maker of sexual desire, according to the ancient Greeks. Did this same intuited feeling of insecurity caused by the possible intrusion of another female into her mate's life stimulate my wife's hypothalamus to produce more oxytocin, that intimacy hormone? Or was my sensorial system being heightened by Mantuo Luo? Did my Chinese masseuse vivify my skin, refining my tactile connection, invigorating my nerve endings?

The Jealous Gods

Alvard Norst was my friend. With a face right out of Wagner's *Ring of the Nibelung*, Alvard looked like a hero from a Nordic saga. He hovered over my life like an albatross over a lost sailboat.

At the age of thirteen, this young Norwegian boy adorned the walls of his room with posters of Dizzy Gillespie and John Coltrane. Alvard was an aficionado of black pornography. On the wall across his bed, he had framed a signed photograph of Jeannie Pepper, who had appeared in *Chocolate Delights, Anal Innocence, Black Taboo, In and Out of Africa*. Every morning he'd masturbate to Jeannie's breast. His movie collection favored black exploitation films like *I'm Gonna Get You Sucka, Across 110th Street, Black Heat, Coonskin,* and *Foxy Brown*. Restless in his native village of Tromso, two hundred miles inside the Arctic Circle, this son of a fisherman bought a one-way ticket to New York. He boarded the USS *Constitution*, a drakkar of steel, for a maritime trek to the New World. Instead of seven hours by plane, Alvard, a true Viking, opted for a sea voyage, seven days in the North Atlantic crossing, fighting gales and squalls.

Black girls and jazz had lured him to the New World. This silver-blond-haired youth with iceberg-blue eyes waited on tables at *Birdland Jazz Club*. He befriended musicians and became a protégé of New York's jazz elite. They had never seen a whiter man than Alvard Norst.

Imitating the lifestyle of the musicians he revered, he began playing the saxophone, using cannabis then cocaine, and became an addict. An overdose sent him to the emergency room at Good Samaritan Hospital, in Suffern, New York. As soon as he was released, he abused the drug again a second time and was committed again. While in detox, wrestling with dragons, he fell in love with his rehabilitation therapist. She was a black girl with an archetypal face who could have modeled for the best sculptor from Benin. She had a name right out of Greek mythology, Ariadne. Didn't Ariadne guide Theseus out of the labyrinth? And with her assistance, didn't he slaughter the Minotaur? Alvard, like his Nordic forebears, was superstitious particularly at the tender age of nineteen. He interpreted his encounter with Ariadne as an omen. He would slay the opiate monster that held him captive and sail in into the moonlit fjord with his paramour.

They rented an efficiency studio in Astoria. He supported himself by playing the saxophone in jazz clubs. Their idyllic romance blossomed. He was happy with his Ariadne. But the gods are envious of mortals, and they are known to sow discord and consternation among the living who experience joy.

A routine medical checkup revealed a lesion in the occipital lobe. Few months later, Ariadne died. To fight death, he registered for medical school. He was an exceptional student. Many reputed hospitals invited to join their staff. He chose Good Samaritan, where years ago he'd been treated for his substance abuse. That's where we met.

While writing this blurb about my friend, the phone rang. It was him. Dining at a Moroccan restaurant near the UN, he had met a Moroccan woman. She was a journalist, a dissident. *The flavor of the week*, I thought.

Leda and the Swan

Melisande Kenworth was the heiress to Horizon Luxury Hotels with 652 resorts in the Caribbeans, Brazil, Thailand, and India. This twenty-seven-year-old single girl with Celtic eyes and manganese-ore-red hair was rushed in the emergency clinic with acute abdominal pain. I relieved her strangulated intestines and added many years to her glamorous life. She became my lover, *une amante*, like the French say. One Saturday, she invited me to the ballet. A dance company from Chicago was interpreting *Swan Lake*. Seats had been reserved months in advance for this event. Melisande called the theater manager and got us tickets.

The audience comprised the elite of New York society. Melisande was greeted by dignitaries.

The swans didn't fly. The prima ballerina was all technique sans ame. Her anorectic body left me listless. I surveyed the troupe with my binoculars. The second from the left was as a woman in an art that neutered the female body. She had breasts and thighs. She had hips.

"The second girl from the right, right?" Melisande whispered.

Women know when their man has spotted their rival.

We left the theater, and her chauffeur dropped us at Karumazushi, where the ingredients are flown straight from Japan. When I realized Melisande was falling in love with me, I spent less time with her. She tried to revive my interest by offering me a Lamborghini. I wasn't to be auctioned.

That night, I checked the dramatis persona in the playbill. The second swan from the left had a Dutch name: Maren Van Devere. I imagined having an affair with her, eager for a private performance. I never fucked a swan, but Leda did. I did nothing about it. Months passed.

Hamburgers for Insomniacs

One evening after our shift at the hospital, Alvard invited me to *The Blue Note*. He was going to be the surprise guest appearance that night.

It was a full house at the jazz club. A jubilant crowd gathered to celebrate the end of the workweek. I colonized a small area at the bar and ordered a drink. I was sipping my Scotch, enjoying Alvard's virtuoso rendering of Sydney Bechet's "Petite Fleur," when the door to the club opened and two girls made their entrance. They were in the midst of a vivid conversation. I notice one of them was limping. I turned to the couple at my side and offered a hundred dollars if they could surrender their barstools. I gestured the two girls to join me. They were surprised a little but took the bait. We talked about European and Japanese jazz compared to American jazz. I bought drinks, mimosas for her, screwdrivers for her friend. Her name was Maren. She was originally from Chicago.

I asked her if burgers are in her gastronomic menu, because I knew this 24-7 joint that makes the best burgers this side of the Mississippi. She'd love to, but she couldn't abandon her friend.

"Let's invite her," I said.

"What kind of a surgeon are you?" Maren asked, looking at my police surgeon decal on my windshield.

"The one who goes in and out without triggering the alarm."

The Wyoming Bar and Grill was bustling. Night insomniacs were biting into garnished burgers with melted, moldy Stilton oozing out of the patties. We ordered decadent burgers and drank Modelos. She was a ballet dancer. Her career was interrupted by a New York finest in hot pursuit of a carjacker. The police cruiser missed a turn and crashed. She wouldn't dance again. Her ambitions had been shattered by an overzealous cop. Her bones were reconstructed with tungsten rods. She could never grace the stage in *Swan Lake* again. Facing this personal apocalypse, she didn't resort to alcohol or drugs, illegal or medicinal. She didn't regress into a post-traumatic limbo. She accepted her fate and, spurred by her love for dance, taught that art in city schools, enriching the life of inner-city children.

Why did I marry an invalid? To bolster my sense of superiority, to prove to my contemporaries I wasn't heir to the vanity of the times? The reason is simple and would challenge the skeptics. I loved her.

Julianne and the Muons

My daughter Julianne is a graduate student in physics. She splits matter in magnetic chambers. She travels in the subatomic world. She's writing a thesis on muons: those ghosts that inhabit the atom's nucleus. Her home away from her is in the Columbia University physics laboratory. She has a relationship with the particles accelerator. She studies entities in motion, stalks their trajectories, photographs their crashes. The collider is a smash palace. Sex, which is a collision, a slamming of bodies in space, she avoids. She prefers the mating dance of subatomic nodules.

I was waiting for her in a booth at Florian's on Park Avenue. She arrived twenty minutes late. She looked overstressed, underfed.

"I haven't had a full meal for weeks," she said, throwing her knapsack on the seat.

There was something profoundly sad about her, something broken.

"How are you?"

"I've been downgraded. My adviser cut into my time with Chris," she said.

"Who's Chris?" I asked.

"The new particles accelerator."

"Why did your adviser do that?" I asked.

"I'm no longer competent to manage Chris. I disturb its magnetic field, says my adviser."

"Chris is a contraption, an appliance. Let's not give feelings to machines," I said.

"We used to have a relationship. He knows I'm not well. He feels the disturbance in the field. He wants my full attention."

"He feels rejected?"

"He's not responding the way he used to. The cyclotron picks up the isotope field around my body."

"Your machine has emotions?"

"He can feel my detachment."

"What are you saying? He…he's in love?"

"He's become…attached."

"Do you love him?"

"Well, yes. Love is an energy field. And I work with energy particles."

There was something somber, suppressed, reserved about her.

"Two weeks ago, I went for a physical. I have ovarian cancer," she said.

"Damn it!" I suppressed the cry.

"Chris knew that. That's why he backed away."

"That's crazy!"

"I don't want to tell Mom. Please, promise me. It's going to be taken care of. I'm having a hysterectomy next Tuesday. It's scheduled."

"Can I talk to the doctor?"

"No, I don't want you involved. I know what I'm doing. Please!"

"Who's the surgeon? Can you tell me his name? I want to be sure you're in good hands."

"Dr. Huy Liang, at NYU Langone Center."

"I know him. He's good."

"Please don't tell Mom."

"I want to visit you at the hospital."

"Sure. Thanks, Dad. Let's eat."

She ordered sea bass with asparagus.

We ate silently. Was Chris the cyclotron responsible for my daughter's cancer? Julianne worked at close proximity to that linear accelerator. Inside that tubular metal corridor, the fission of subatomic particles radiated waves. Julianne's body was permeated by by-products of these atomic explosions. Magnetic pollution was a hazard. Radiation permeated every employee, yet no protective gear is worn by technicians and scientists.

"Is it safe—I mean, spending all that time with Chris?" I asked.

"The fission of particles is enclosed and insulated."

"How about leakages? There are cracks in every insulation?"
"Dad, cancer is genetic, not environmental."
"Radiation affects genes. They mutate."
"My grandmother died of ovarian cancer."
"Yes, at eighty-five. You're twenty-six years old."
"I'll be fine. They'll remove the cancer cells. I'll be fine."
"You told me that 99 percent of matter is a void."
"Yes, an ocean of emptiness," she said.
"You love that emptiness."
"Maybe that's where it all started. God is emptiness," Julianne said.
"Well, that's comforting."
"You know, Dad, you might think that that 99 percent void is dark, absolutely black. But it isn't. It's colorless, really. That 1 percent is conceived in an achromatic expanse. Knowing that we are 99 percent void is reassuring, Dad."

Julianne understood what we all want to forget, that we are at the fringe of nothingness.

"The last words of Goethe in his dying bed: *Mehr licht! More light!* I've got a gift for you," she said, picking up her knapsack.

It was a book gift wrapped in iridescent paper. *Freud: Living and Dying* by Max Shur.

"He was his private doctor, Dad."
"Thank you."
"I've started psychoanalytic psychotherapy."
"Oh?"
"I don't know what to make of this tumor? Why my reproductive organs? It sucks!" she lamented.
"You said it was genetic."
"I know."

My daughter will never pass her genetic signature to future generations. She was my only offspring, my biological heiress. That ends my bloodline.

"I'll never have children. Maybe it's better that way. I read that couples reproduce out of despair. They're crushed by their own insignificance, so they decide to make children. That's how the species multiplies. It's sad," she said.

"We didn't feel despair when we conceived you," I interjected.

"Infants are vampires, narcissistic larvae that suck their mother's blood and milk. I'm glad I'll be sterile."

"Don't say that."

"Come on, Dad, wasn't I a brat at two?"

"You were fascinated by balloons floating in the ceiling of your room. Already an astrophysicist."

Julianne sipped her coffee.

"What I don't understand is why target the reproductive organs? Doesn't nature want more of itself? It's sabotaging itself," she protested.

"Good question!"

"I talked about it to my therapist. He told me about a paper Freud wrote in 1920: *Beyond the Pleasure Principle*. He said there might be a silent drive towards death, a secret desire for annihilation, a longing for extinction, an attraction towards our own end. He called it the death instinct."

"Well, you know, sometimes I'm doing surgery, and all is going well. I'm at the top of my game, and the patient is holding his own. And then, just like that, everything starts to go wrong. The guy on the surgical table is in the grip of a death-life struggle. Is he fighting some invisible force that our scanners can't detect? I don't know. He dies on the surgical table."

"Freud was addicted to cigars. He smoked twenty cigars a day. He had thirty-three surgical operations performed on his mouth. He refused painkillers. He wouldn't stop smoking, which aggravated the wound in his palate. He saw his cancer as the working of the death instinct. He was romantic about death. He said he welcomed the transition to nonbeing. Pretty fucked up!" Julianne said.

"Did he find out why he smoked so many cigars?"

"He said smoking was a substitute for kissing, a substitute for a good lay. Funny thing, he was a puritan who brought sexual consciousness to neurology. He never visited a brothel in Vienna which was famous all over Europe for its prostitutes."

"You're so smart!" I said.

"And what did it do for me, Dad?"

"Everything, Julie!"

Julianne D'Arcy was born in December under the sign of Sagittarius, whatever that means.

I remember her mother and I were lounging on the blue sofa in the living room, watching a French horror movie, *Diabolique*. The contractions began at 11:47 p.m. We drove to NYU Hospital from Westchester. I feared her water would break and she'd deliver in the back seat of the Mercedes. We were in the emergency room by 12:45 a.m. It was a Caesarean delivery, painless but bloody.

At the age of five, Julianne was intrigued by color and light, the silhouette of her toys on walls, the yellow of sunrays. She'd spend hours peeping through the aperture of a kaleidoscope. She'd steal my glasses and place them in the trajectory of a sunbeam to project a spectrum on the opposite wall. She'd check the weather channel, hoping for a summer rainfall to glimpse at a rainbow in the sky. It didn't take long for her teachers to realize she was an exceptional pupil. In high school, she became interested in infrared energy, photons, x-rays, etc. Her passion for light had reached scientific proportions. She had amassed flawless grades semester after semester and was awarded a bountiful postgraduate scholarship, all expenses paid, at Columbia University. At night, she'd hang out at the lab not in bars or clubs. But one day at the library, she spotted a nymphet.

"What're you writing?" she asked.

"An essay on Euler's identity."

Love at the first equation. Julianne had found her alter ego, her double. She invited Ulia for a meet-my-parents dinner. She was a Finnish Lolita with eyes that could melt glaciers and a sharp chin she inherited from arctic wolves. Her angular face recalled Baudelaire's saying that *the beautiful is bizarre by definition*. Ulia's mother was toiling at the UN, assigned to write policy and strategy to eliminate sexual slave trade among Islamic groups in the Middle East. Julianne and Ulia played house on 116th Street and Broadway, a studio Julianne painted navy blue. Through Ulia, Julianne had uncovered the mysteries of her body. Ulia transformed my daughter into a mass of sensations, a crescendo of major chords. At the height of her passion, Julianne had discovered Baroque music: Purcell, Corelli,

Monteverdi, Pachelbel, Lully, Rameau, Albinoni, Couperin. The Baroque style, she asserted, was nuclear physics in musical form. It had repetition, harmony and counterpoint, basso. Under Julianne's radar, the blond elf from Helsinki (elves are associated with sexual threats, seducing innocents and causing them harm) was sucking her fractals professor's dick after class in the unlit, empty auditorium. The professor, unhinged by that Finnish pussy, dumped his wife and three underage children for the Nordic fairy.

Ulia and the professor eloped, precipitating a scandal in the mathematics department, challenging the theory of probability, which is the analysis of random events. Julianne took this catastrophe with aplomb, at least in the surface of things. Outwardly, she exhibited no visible turbulence. Her innate ability for abstract processing saved the day. She buried herself in her work, that subatomic realm of possibilities. She delved deeper into atomic nuclei and their constituents. She had found refuge and sanctuary in the company of muons. In the collider of her unconscious, she bombarded the Ulia entity, pulverizing that quantity into smithereens. Julianne survived this natural disaster. Two years after this upheaval, she received a handwritten envelope with a stamp from Bora Bora. Ulia and her new Maori husband were running a bed-and-breakfast for European and American surfers. It was an apology, belated. She was making amends. Julianne didn't write back.

Rebellious Flesh

Walking away from the liquor store with a bottle of Riesling, my penis contorted like a heated rubber hose (damn thing never followed instructions). I sat in my car for a few minutes consoling my rebellious flesh.

That night, the air in Chelsea stank of body lotion and Red Bull. My sense of smell was becoming more acute. These aromas didn't affect my breathing. My lungs inhaled the rancid air without complaint.

The elevator to the ninth floor moaned with a loud metallic cough.

The pickled Chinese madam ushered me to the massage room and brought a teapot. The flavored steam from the jasmine tea scented the room.

I uncorked the bottle and poured the wine in two porcelain cups decorated with dragons. Her thin fingers wrapped around the glass as if it were a chalice.

"Wine," I pronounced several times. She repeated the word. Didn't she recruit clients at the AA meetings she attended? In her dealings with alcoholics, she must have encountered countless names of fermented and distilled spirits.

Heavy emotions seemed to rise from her body like vapors off a lake in the chilly morning air. With one finger, she brushed against the back of my neck. Vertigo, as if the earth's axis had been altered. The tilt of my planet was recorded by a mudded brain. How could two glasses of wine affect my gyroscope so dramatically?

She worked on the neck muscles unraveling ancient Gordian Knot embedded in the deep tissues, nodules of twisted nerves in the musculature. With full hands, she expanded the cellular netting, prolonging its architecture.

Walking toward the car, I reflected on this last session and the impact of the wine on her mood and mine. How could I be so naive thinking I was introducing her to Western alcoholic beverages? Wasn't she ministering her skills on veteran drinkers encountered in sobriety meetings?

*****

Back in the internet café, huddled in her polyurethane seat, Maren pressed the Pause button. The thought of her husband drinking wine with another woman unhinged her. Wine was an elixir she shared with her oenophile husband. In her mind, shadows began to bloom like a squid's ink in water. She needed a sharp drink to dissolve the shards of pain. She unplugged the drive.

She walked out of the internet café and wandered around town seeking a bar. *Antrim* was almost empty that time of the day. The afternoon regulars, retired citizens were sipping their beer and watching a baseball game on the flat-screen TV. She ordered a Rémy Martin. Within minutes, she could feel the analgesic effect. She refilled her tumbler. Sedation was welcomed. But loss of lucidity she didn't want. She traipsed back to the internet café and slipped her drive in the USB outlet.

Words that Heal

I wanted her to acquire a vocabulary. She was not eager to speak the language of the host country. She opted for taciturnity. Language is not only essential for intimacy, but also it compensates for the inadequacy of remedies and cures for most diseases.

She wrote in her phone in Mandarin a few lines which her electronic dictionary translated.

I wrote my response, a few English sentences on my phone which were translated in Mandarin. I was finding her position regressive. She responded, "*Speech destroys, when it's all that remains between a man and a woman, that relationship is over.*"

I got dressed hurriedly and left the salon. Darkened by her anti-literary position, I was wishing a termination to this odd association.

I resented Mantuo Luo's illiteracy. I resisted the silent magnetism that kept me in her ellipse like an asteroid pulled by the gravitational force of a planet, forcing it to orbit endlessly until the degradation of that trajectory coerces the savage reentry of that astral body into the atmosphere of that host planet and its final disintegration as it rushes mindlessly and crashing on an inhospitable surface.

I felt that Mantuo Luo had placed our relationship inside a straitjacket.

I was driving across the Tappan Zee Bridge when the nausea overtook me. A scent of honey and organic decay invaded me. I felt like I was breathing the air inside an equatorial greenhouse, rotting leafing plants putrefying. The odor lingered then suddenly vanished.

Pygmalion

The interior of *Cuchulain's* was cedar and mahogany. I cozied inside a booth and ordered a whiskey. The television screen was pulsating. Advertisements were flashing the new spring fashions. Sluttishness was in style this season: skintight shorts, cutoff T-shirts, ripped jeans, yoga pants, camel toes.

I phoned Alvard.

Alvard had new monikers for me: *Professor Higgins* from *My Fair Lady* and *Pygmalion* from that ancient Greek tale.

"Are you falling in love with your Galatea?" he asked.

"I'm not falling."

"You like her tight lychee cunt, don't you?"

"Don't go there!" I snapped.

I realized I had to firm up the boundaries with my Chinese therapist. Does "relationship" define a liaison between patient/client and health provider? Is it a bond, an affinity, an alliance? No word defined this barter between me and Mantuo Luo. Was it an affair, a partnership? Patients nurture feelings for their doctor. I benefited from those attachments. Freud called it transference, a stimulus that assists and supports the healing process.

"I haven't set foot in her massage parlor for fifty three days," I blurted.

"Counting the days, I see," he struck.

"I'm avoiding her."

"You can always try," he replied.

He hang up.

I've been listening to *Madame Butterfly* and *Turandot*. These two operas narrate the passion of two Asian women for Western men.

I kept phoning Alvard, hoping to get absolution. I was making a mistake in pursuing him. He was becoming my rival. He wouldn't be my redeemer. I felt like a sea captain without his sextant.

I got to talk to him.

"Go visit another massage establishment and get the complete treatment this time, full service," he recommended boldly.

"You're trying to sabotage my relationship with Mantuo Luo," I said.

"You don't have a relationship. You're a client, only a client."

"I'm more than a client," I dared.

"You need to imagine her rubbing the sweaty, pungent dorsal vertebrae of some blue-collar worker on disability. That would cure you of any romantic delusion."

"Stop it!"

"Go to that other kind of body-rub establishment. Explore the pleasures of the Orient right here in Chinatown. Be unfaithful to her. Break the curse!"

Alvard was an agent provocateur fomenting a mutiny. He had patronized her in the past. Her hands caressed his pale, lusterless albino Nordic skin. He was still scheduling sessions with her. The image of her fingers surfing through his blanched epidermis nauseated me.

When I arrived home, my wife was conducting a yoga class in her new studio in the attic. I sat on the lounge chair in the patio with a notepad. I'd write a letter to Mantuo Luo. What would I write? What did I know about this woman? I was uninformed about her culture, illiterate: a barbarian at the gate of the Forbidden City.

For the next days, I immersed myself in the acquisition of knowledge, devoured cultural records. I explored the court music of the Han, Tang, Ming, and Manchu dynasties. I excavated the underlying stratas that defined Chinese identity.

Her interpretation of the world was different from mine. Only frail bridges could be built between these two distant shores. I'd be prospecting in the quarry of her soul, like an archaeologist on a mission to identify a buried city through artifacts embedded in the soil. I'd never exhaust the myriad of relics my shovel will exhume.

Getting to know her ethnic identity excited me. I was Heinrich Schliemann excavating the site of Troy. Mantuo Luo was the heiress to that culture I was going to uncover. But to me, she was essentially a stranger. Baudelaire was right: *"We love women in proportion to their degree of strangeness to us."*

I discovered Chinese cinema. I watched *The Curse of the Golden Flower*. The costumes, decors, gardens of the Tang dynasty enchanted me, and the face of Gong Li and her grace and elegance enraptured me. I watched *Hero* directed by Zhang Yimou about the assassination attempt on the tyrant king of Qin Shi Huang in 227 BC. The psychology of the assassins was not occidental and couldn't be fathomed by an American mind. I enjoyed *The House of The Flying Daggers*, by Zhang Yimou: the tale of a blind woman who is adored by two men who fight for her to the bitter end.

Illiteracy was the by-product of Mao Zedong's paranoia of the intellectuals. Mantuo had been the victim of a regime governed by the son of a peasant who hated the educated classes. With Mao, that rage of the farmers against the urban classes blossomed. Her parents belonged to that educated urban class.

I encountered the pervading force of Chinese isolationism. How Emperor Kang Hsi answered Louis XIV's letter of offering French science to the Manchu court by saying to the Sun King that China didn't need anything from France.

I read about Western prejudices toward the Asiatic races: the European disdain of Imperial China. How twice the English forced the Chinese to purchase opium, the explosion of the Boxer Rebellion fueled by Chinese activists who tried to liberate their seaports from European businessmen, the Imperial attempts to restrict the poisonous proliferation of European Christianity on the naive souls of the Chinese farmers. The psychotic conversion of a farmer Hong Xiaqua who had failed four times the Imperial exam. Unable to find employment in the Imperial court, he was transformed, after listening to a sermon by a proselytizing Anglican minister. Armed by a sudden revelation from Jesus himself that he was his brother, he lit upon Manchu China the fires of the Taiping rebellion, which burned for fifteen years and left thirty millions dead Chinese.

Will I dare to remind Mantuo of Mao Zedong's subjugation of her free will, the Great Famine where millions of her countrymen died of hunger due to his agricultural policies? This event must have affected the lives of her parents. I calculated she must have been around nine years old during the Cultural Revolution. I speculated she'd arrived in New York, a refugee who entered the country on a political asylum visa.

The Yoga Sanctuary

I joined my wife's yoga class on Wednesday evenings at 7:00 p.m. I climbed the set of stairs to the refurbished attic. Incense sticks fumigated the space.

Students stared at me. They were local housewives and daughters from our town. My wife announced she wanted them to focus on a particular yoga stance, concentrate on an *asana*, yoga lingo for the pose *downward-facing dog*. It sounded like a sexual position from the *Kama Sutra*. She pronounced the name of that asana in Hindi to give it legitimacy: *adho mukha svanasana*. "Tuck toes up and lift hips up," she instructed as she strolled, correcting protruding hips, reshaping anatomies in distress. I coerced my reluctant body to obey the instructor's order, twisting my musculature to fulfill her command. I couldn't perform this pose for a million dollars in African diamonds. Yet yoga provided a momentary lull in my craving, an interval.

I attended the yoga classes with regularity. I had a nonflexible body. I observed that after class, my spirit soared beyond the gravitational pull of my depression. My wife approached me. She witnessed my body struggle with another designed-in-hell asana. She patted my shoulder and smiled.

A Sea Mollusk

As I was walking the streets of Manhattan, illuminated advertisement boards adorned facades of the remaining brick-stone buildings in a city where skyscrapers are built every month. Where to find a classy establishment where clients are treated like shoguns, not unemployed samurais?

I voyaged through the continent of the internet and, in my wanderings, discovered *an online magazine.* Ads filled the screen of my iPad, images of massage parlors. The masseuses had names like Koko, Jade, Pearl, Sissy, Cinnabar, Star, Myrrh. Establishments boasted Koreans, Japanese, Chinese, and Thai girls. They promised clients would be treated like honored guests, treasured visitors. I felt like a European sailor in the Red District of Old Shanghai visiting the lavish brothels, lairs of sultry courtesans.

I chose a Japanese establishment that highlighted in its website the painting of *The Wave* by Hokusai. It boasted the words "Come and live the dream of the Orient." It felt like an advertisement for a tourist's tour promotion. The madam flaunted the loveliness of Inagaki, a new girl who had just landed in New York a month ago from Nagasaki. She had studied English in her native city and could speak, but her hands could sing.

I parked on Thirty-Second between Fifth and Sixth Avenue, the heart of Korea Town. An aroma of boiled cabbage, garlic-marinated pork, and roasted coconut scented the air. Asian bakeries, pastry shops, restaurants with fluorescent signs boasting Korean culinary delights illuminated the street. Pavements were crowded with throngs of patrons lined up outside eating establishments. Women gathered at the entrance of boutiques, faces like bouquets. The women were petite, slim, dainty. Luminous eyes with straight cascading anthracite hair displayed diminutive sculpted mouths with glistening lips. Their accent was musical, their voices melodious disrupted by peals of laughter like the resonance of colliding chimes.

The sign on the elevator door read "not working." I climbed the stairs. Breathless.

A Japanese print illustrating a winter scene with Mount Fuji in the horizon garnished the door, a fitting advertisement for a travel agency.

A matronly madam with a face like a steamed dumpling greeted me. She escorted me to a massage room lit by a blue lantern. The room was tiny. A black kimono was hanging on a brass hook.

The room smelled of strawberry and sandalwood. I thought that by invading that hidden orifice in the body of another Asian woman, travel deep in her being, I'd walk away with something rare and transubstantial, the cure to my addiction to Mantuo Luo.

Inagaki's face conjured floral images. She was ginger blossom, tea petal, freshwater pearl. Her body contoured a slinky fuchsia dress. In the midst of my elation, dreadful images intruded, shattering my euphoria. Burning bodies were running in the streets of Nagasaki, skinned alive by the atmospheric blast. I imagined that at 1:56 a.m. on August 9, 1945, her grandparents were asleep on flower-print futons on wooden floors when the sky brightened like a thousand suns. Did she know who Captain Charles Sweeney was?

"My name is Inagaki," she whispered, bowing.

"My name is Tokugawa," I said.

She burst out laughing. I had offered the name of the warlord who united Japan after years of civil wars.

She undressed languidly, sumptuously exposing her pale body. She was made of the finest stuff: ebony, alabaster, porcelain, the purest silk. The face of an Oriental Madonna. I was a pearl fisherman opening a sea mollusk prospecting for the elusive jewel. Like the octopus shucking a clam, my lips, tongue, and teeth foraged inside the meaty crustacean. She was eager to return the pleasure. I gently declined. My conscience wouldn't allow further rapture. I was due for an auto-da-fé.

I was laden with despair. My liaison with Mantuo Luo had opened the gate to a deeper longing. I thought of Schopenhauer and

Nietzsche, Alvard's favorite philosophers, who spoke best of love, yet each one frequented brothels their whole life. I understood their choices. It was simpler, and preferable, to reduce the longings of the heart to a physical embrace. Regrettably, I realized that no other woman could erase Mantuo Luo's indelible presence.

I was getting dressed when a knock on the door jarred the silence of the moment.

"Open up!" the man's voice reverberated.

The burly detective in jeans and plaid lumberjack shirt flashed his police badge.

"Get dressed," he ordered.

He knocked on other doors, interrupting coitus in progress.

I felt like an impaled fish.

I joined the other patrons in the waiting room. They looked guilty, trapped.

The masseuses lined up against the wall.

"Who did you give the house fee to?" the burly man asked.

I didn't answer.

"There's a licensing problem with this establishment," he explained.

It was an excuse to collect the cash the masseuses had collected on that workday. It was legalized extortion. The madam hadn't paid her protection money for the month. The cops were in on it.

"You're free to go," the detective said.

I was filled with rage at the subterfuge beneath it all. I predicted the joint would reopen in a few hours. The next day, I called to check Inagaki's availability for an 11:00 p.m. session. Without hesitation, the madam booked me for that night slot. I never went.

*****

Maren pressed the Pause button. Her husband's sexual delinquency started a forest fire in her. Gabriel had become a visitor of bordellos that camouflaged as massage spas. Her mind traveled to their early romance, a period of rapture and felicity. The reverie into yesterday evaporated into a repugnant present. She pressed the Enter button.

*****

My wife had prepared Lapin à la Moutarde. I was anxious during dinner, inward. Alvard was the guardian of my secret. Although I could count on his discretion in this matter, I felt unbalanced by his presence in my home. I was distracted, opaque, an imperfect host, seeking the sanctuary of the kitchen. He had brought with him a woman. I forced myself to join the party.

"It's a work of art, your lapin," Alvard praised.

"Thank you for inviting me," Farhana said.

Maren was studying Farhana's face, the bronze of her skin, the ochre hue of her eyes.

"May I have some ice?" Farhana asked.

"Of course," Maren said.

"Please don't get up. I'll go get it."

Farhana was wearing pants so tight I could tell the exact place her thighs began that sublime division. Into the pants was tucked a close-fitting turquoise blouse.

She returned with ice in a bowl.

"You're a yoga teacher?" Farhana asked Maren.

"Yes. Have you ever taken a yoga class?"

"Yes, at the Bikram Yoga Center."

"That's when they heat the room until you sweat like a galley slave," Alvard advanced.

"When muscles are heated, they become elastic," Farhana said.

"Bikram got into trouble, I recall," I said.

"Why is it gurus molest their devotees? They live like Mughal emperors on our dime and fuck our girls, often underage too," Alvard mouthed.

"Is that true?" I asked.

"Maharishi Mahesh Yogi, the guru for the Beatles and the Beach Boys in the sixties. He introduced transcendental meditation to the West and became a millionaire. His devotees referred to him as

His Holiness. And then the Beatles find out he was fucking the girls from the ashram. Chandra Mohan Jain, a.k.a. Rajneesh, was the sex guru. He owned a fleet of Rolls-Royces. His devotees bought him a sixty-four thousand acres property in Oregon and built an ashram. He broke so many laws of the land, clashed against US authorities who finally evicted him back to India. Twenty-one countries denied him entry. Muktananda appealed to a lot of Hollywood types with deep pockets. His fans bought him land in upstate New York for his ashram. They tried to squelch the scandal that he was fucking teenage girls. Indian mystics come to America to fuck and make money. That's because sex in India is essentially taboo. Spirituality has strangulated the genitals of millions of Indians. It's a country of vegetarian farmers ruled by a castrated theocracy," Farhana launched.

I was impressed by her bravado.

"You're a journalist. What do you write about?" I asked.

"Current affairs, lifestyle, social media, and the contemporary woman."

"What do women want?" I asked.

"Brand names, Louis Vuitton, Hermes, etc. They want to marry a hedge fund millionaire and cheat with Hispanic trainers. In comparison, Asian women want to settle down with a man who has a steady job," Farhana said.

"Are you writing about the new sexual revolution?" Alvard asked.

"Of course. Chat rooms, Tinder, Bumble, Happen. Instant gratification. It's disposable sex. What happened to food has happened to sex. Fast food, food to go, expendable plastic cups, usable, throwaways. It's single-use sex. Pornography is global and employs millions of women who are making a living thanks to the internet. Girls are illiterate in Third World countries. To survive in a male-dominated planet, they cater to men who run the machinery of society. Nudity becomes a global presence. Our world has become ocular. Men covet. Teenage boys don't steal *Playboy* magazines anymore at the local grocery store. They don't raid *Penthouse* magazines in the locked drawer in their father's closet. They access pornographic sites and masturbate to videos of MILFs," Farhana said.

"What happened to love?" Maren asked.

"A business transaction, a barter?" Farhana said.

"There's a movement to ban pornography from the internet. That's what they did to alcohol during the Prohibition. These anti-sex groups are run by women," I ventured.

"'You know what the suffragettes deserve? The whip and the harem,' that's what Colette said," Farhana mouthed.

"Colette wrote a book on gender identity, *The Pure and the Impure*. She says that forbidden desires, when they go underground, resurface later as perversions," Alvard said.

"That's pure Freud," I commented.

"Before the internet, we had the personals," Alvard echoed.

"I picked up a copy of *The New York Review of Books* when I wanted to meet an intellectual girl," I ventured.

"Did you?" my wife asked.

"That's how I met Phaedra."

"Phaedra. I love that name," Alvard beamed. "That was Ariadne's sister. Theseus dumped Ariadne, who helped him kill the Minotaur and ran away with her sister, Phaedra. You were dating Phaedra, and I was dating Ariadne. That's wild!" Alvard beamed.

"Were you fond of her?" my wife asked.

"She was a flight attendant. She'd disappear for weeks, traveled all over the world. I think on layovers, she was fucking members of the flight crew."

"She must have had other talents," Maren said.

"Her body was a buffet. It was self-service, only."

"How about you?" Alvard turned to Maren.

"Theo, from Iowa. Came to New York City to study journalism. Sweet guy," Maren said dreamily.

"What did he write about?" Alvard asked.

"He was writing an article on the Second Avenue Subway fiasco. Twenty years they've been working on it, digging the tunnel, and millions of dollars later, nada. He named some people he thought responsible for that debacle. He was hit by a cabdriver from Bangladesh. Theo was a bike rider."

"Easy target," Farhana said.

"What do you mean?" Maren asked.
"You think it was an accident?" Farhana dropped.
"It was an accident. I'm sure of it?"
"What happened to the cabdriver?"
"They couldn't find him."
"Of course! He's in Bangladesh living the life."
"If Theo hadn't been run over by a Moslem taxi driver from Bangladesh doing a double shift, I wouldn't have met Maren."
"How about some coffee, strictly organic beans?" Maren announced.

Maren returned from the kitchen with a large coffeepot and cups.

"Do you have good memories, about your childhood?" I asked Farhana.

"My father was a manager of a beach hotel in Djerba, a resort town in Tunisia. An anonymous letter was hand delivered, warning that if tourists continued bathing in the nude, there'd be hell to pay. He wasn't about starting to restrict the French girls from bathing naked. He knew an Islamic group was responsible for the note. He informed the police. Plainclothes officers patrolled the grounds. At dusk, the dining room was full. The show was in progress. A belly dancer was entertaining the tourists. I was in the kitchen making pistachio cookies. The earth shook. The nails ripped lungs, arms, and legs. They found my father's head in the pool. Mother decided to leave Tunisia. My mother went to the American embassy. She wanted a political asylum visa. There were forms to fill, phone calls to make, errands to departmental offices. I'd come home from school, and I'd find her sobbing. I was sixteen years old. I bought a black dress, black stockings. At the desk at the embassy, I said I had an appointment with Mr. Hutchinson, the assistant to the station chief. The clerk checked the appointment list. He couldn't find my name. I whispered that it wasn't an official visit and that my name wouldn't appear in any list. The clerk's face became red. Mr. Hutchinson was a bureaucrat doing his tour of duty in the foreign office. You have to go through the proper channels," he said.

"I told him my mother has been in the embassy seven times. My father had been killed by Islamic militants. 'Give me your tired, your poor, your huddled masses yearning to breathe free, the wretched refuse of your teeming shore. Send these, the homeless, tempest-tossed, to me. I lift my lamp beside the gold door,' I recited the words of Emma Lazarus. I fell on my knees. I begged. With my teeth, I unzipped his trousers. His cock looked like a bleached carrot. I was bobbing my head, pumping his thing. He had iguana eyes. I took a selfie with his cock in my mouth and his face looking terrified. I left, my heart beating like a Bedouin drum. Two days later, a messenger delivered an official envelope with the seal of the United States of America. I walked in the kitchen and showed the visas to my mother."

Maren was dazed. Alvard applauded.

"My people were scientists, poets, architects, engineers. Islam crushed everything. They haven't invented anything since they started to listen to Mohammed. Our desert has produced nothing but lunatics and half-wits. Where the Crusades failed, now the West has a chance to crush Islam for good."

"How's that?" Maren asked.

"Islam promises forty juicy virgins whose skin is so pale you can see the veins, arteries, and bones. I'm quoting the Quran, no joke. Mohammed offered every Moslem in the afterlife his own brothel. But now, Moslems don't have to go to the afterlife to join an orgy. They can book a trip to the Philippines or Thailand and get laid. Or if they don't have the money, they can go in the internet and watch a teenager in Liverpool remove her panties, and they can jerk off to her Celtic pussy. That's the greatest threat to Islam: ready and available sex. They can't fight that. The fundamentalists, they're really scared. Mohammed Atta, the guy who masterminded 9/11 was visiting a topless bar before the day of the attack," Farhana said.

"Why didn't he stay alive and buy more lap dances?" Alvard asked.

"Guilt! He couldn't tolerate pleasure on earth. It's defiance against Islam to experience paradise on earth. It's supposed to happen after you die."

I listened to Farhana vividly. She was an intellectual insurgent, an ideological rebel. I was turned on by her mind. I envied Alvard. He was fucking her, and I wondered how she tasted.

I was falling in love with that Berber girl. Farhana was a philosopher, an emancipated Moslem in an age of fatwas.

I imagined Farhana's nude body, lean and tawny, her breasts with sharp nipples, her labias mauve framed by a maroon pudenda. I visualized her clitoris, defiant, triumphant, a minaret darting out from the mosque of her Mount of Venus. The imagery fired up my brain's RPM. My wife, who sensed my delirium, poured me a glass of Pellegrino. I didn't regret my mild inebriation. I was contemplating Farhana's face, remembering Nietzsche's comment about beauty: a promise of happiness. She wasn't a luxury animal. She didn't need to be pampered or spoiled. Her use could be extended beyond fucking. She had a mind that examined the world and wrote about it.

My wife was riveted by Farhana.

"Are you happy in your marriage?" Farhana asked me suddenly.

"Yes," was my immediate response.

"And you have a daughter."

"Yes, Julianne."

"Are you close?"

"Very much."

"How often do you speak?"

"Once a week, at least."

Farhana closed up.

"What's wrong?" Maren asked.

"I will never get married and have children," Farhana announced plaintively.

"Why not?" Maren asked.

"Children drain parents," she protested.

"We have a daughter, and we don't feel drained," Maren said.

"We made a baby because we loved each other," I said.

"City councils should plan for infant-free zones for apartment residents who won't tolerate the crying, whining, the odor of shit and vomit in the lobbies of their buildings," Farhana continued boldly.

"You're for depopulation," I shot back.

"It will redirect resources that are now allocated to newborns. What a waste."

Farhana was a nihilist, a liberated anarchist, a Berber woman emancipated from sixteen centuries of bondage to a desert god and his illiterate prophet.

"I've been thinking of adopting a pet," Maren said, changing the topic. "I've been talking to a breeder upstate."

"Pets are a source of great disillusionment," Farhana snapped.

"I can see that," Alvard said. "You expect them to have a confidential conversation with you, to tell you their secrets, to confide in you. They just stare."

"The rage of slaves simmers in their heart," Farhana said.

"They make good companions," Maren said.

"They're responsible for their servitude. They've seduced us to diversify their breed by genetic manipulation. They've coaxed us to make more of them. They had a plan," Farhana blurted.

"What a grim view," Maren grimaced.

"Do you think plants are guilty of the same crime?" I asked.

"They're worse. They're the ultimate seducers. Plants captured us to expand their breeds. And to have dominion over us. Coffee, tea, apples, tomatoes, potatoes, wheat, rice, cannabis, etc. were scrawny bushes growing in some of the most isolated places on earth until someone discovered them and was seduced. They fed our hunger, stimulated our taste buds, and sedated us. Now, they've conquered the planet, and we are at their service. That's what that great book is about, *The Botany of Desire*."

"What do you recommend?" I asked.

"We return to a purely carnivorous diet," Farhana said defiantly.

She paused and helped herself to a hefty slice of black forest cake.

"Do you like animals?" Farhana turned to Alvard.

"Yes, birds."

"We adopted two finches. Our home was full of songs. And then the songs stopped. Pneumonia. Somebody left the window open," Maren lamented.

"Mea culpa," I said.

"I've recorded songbirds, when I could find them. We didn't have too many songbirds in Norway. What bird in its right mind would make a home in fucking Norway? My dream since I was a kid was to have an aviary with birds from Brazil—you know, from the rain forest," Alvard echoed.

"How'd you get the birds?" asked Maren.

"I'd call breeders in Mexico, Brazil, Sri Lanka, India, Indonesia, and Thailand. They ship eggs internationally now."

A pause in the conversation. Coffee refilled the cups.

"Are you a plastic surgeon?" Farhana asked me.

"No, he's a plastic sturgeon," dropped Alvard.

"Very funny," Maren giggled.

"What're you thinking?" Alvard asked Farhana.

"Labial reconstruction. I have elephant ears. I've been told American men like it streamlined, Anglo-Saxon sensibility," Farhana intoned.

"Yeah? What an Anglo-Saxon pussy looks like?" Alvard asked.

"No ridges, layers, strata, edges, pendulous lips. A minimalist pussy, parallel lines, almost an abstraction of a pussy the opposite of that French pastry mille-feuilles."

"I'm Norwegian. I guess I prefer minimalist pussies," Alvard intoned.

"That explains why you're not enamored with my cunt." Farhana smiled.

"Give me time to adjust," Alvard said, blowing her a kiss.

"My ex-boyfriend had ejaculation issues. I think it's because of my lips. They made him anxious. Too much skin. The only way he came was when I cajoled his balls. He used to say that women he had dated completely ignored his testicles. He happened to have very sensitive balls," Farhana claimed.

"I think women are afraid of testicles," Alvard bellowed.

"Why do you say that?" I asked.

"Women don't want to deal with testicles. When they give blow jobs, all their focus is on sucking cocks. They neglect balls, when they should lick them, envelop them in their mouths, caress them, cuddle them, fondle them, palpate them, stroke them, squeeze them. They forget that's the semen factory. When a man's balls are the focus of his lover's affection, he feels cherished. A man's heart isn't through his stomach as that cliché promises, it's through his balls," Farhana expounded.

I thought of my lovemaking with Maren. My wife catered harmless pleasure to a disciplined man. I accepted her domesticated sex drive and invested my libido in my professional career. In my line of work, opportunities to plant my organ in willing orifices abounded. Patients who lusted after surgeons were legions. As a surgeon, I visited their bodies, palpated organs no lover accessed. I ripped their abdomen open and plunged my fingers in their innards. The surgery, under my supervision, was a success and the prognosis excellent. I had performed my duty with dedication. I didn't seduce these women or profited from their condition. They were grateful for my healing intervention. Their recovered femininity yearned for validation. They wanted to relish a future now made secure by my salutary medical intervention, a future which had been in doubt before the treatment I ministered. I'd sensed their longings but didn't gratify them. The physical love we couldn't share was in complete accord with my ethics.

It was getting late. The party was ending. Alvard said goodbye. Farhana hugged me a bit too tight. She dropped her iPhone as she was exiting. She bent to retrieve it. Because of her tight dress, I could see the knobs on her backbone, a soft rope that disappeared down into the crevice.

I cleared the table.

"What do you think of Farhana?" I asked.

"She's a blowhard!" came the reply.

"Yes, she's exhausting!" I launched.

"She lectures! I hate women who lecture. She's a know-it-all. Can't stand people who flaunt their intelligence. It's a long monologue. No dialogue with that one."

"I agreed. One couldn't have a conversation with that kind of gal."

"She's not your type, honey," Maren countered.

"And what's my type?"

"The nonintellectual type."

"Why do you say that?"

"You told me once, if a man is thinking of marrying an intellectual woman, he should get a subscription to the public library instead."

"I said that?"

"Yes."

"That's a terrible thing to say."

"I married you! I'm not an intellectual. I'm a dancer and a yoga instructor."

"But that's what I loved about you. Through dance and yoga, you ennoble the body. You empower it. I fix it. I'm the mechanic. I'm the repairman. Yeah, we both have this thing for the body. You forgive me?"

"For what?"

"I'm a male narcissistic idiot.'"

"The jury is out deliberating, honey."

"When will the sentence be passed?"

"We'll see. I'm going to bed. That prosecco got the best of me."

She disappeared upstairs. I lingered in the gym downstairs and lit up the TV screen.

A commentator was suggesting pets were taking over. Because of the unconditional love they provide, perpetual good mood, willingness to play anytime of the day, and low maintenance, they'd become the default companion of contemporary men and women. Couples from Atlanta, Chicago, Tokyo, Tel Aviv, Barcelona, Copenhagen testified their willingness to adopt a dog or a cat instead of a human child. They justified their choices on financial grounds too, saying raising a child was becoming an economic challenge. A married captain in the US Air Force was interviewed. The couple loved their German shepherd. It was a part of the family. Accidentally, the captain impregnated his wife. They had a baby girl. It became obvious that this new human arrival in the family didn't please the dog. The German shepherd became depressed. It stopped eating, playing, defecating. The couple put their baby daughter for adoption. They donated their newborn to an agency that provided Caucasian children to sterile American couples. The dog improved. The interviewed couple justified their action. They concluded, given the circumstances, that it was the right thing to do. I wanted to scream, but I was too tired. I fell asleep on the faux leather sofa in the gym.

Choreography of Desire

While contorting my body to accomplish another asana, *paripurna navasana*, my wife stopped the lesson to address her class: "For many weeks, our class has been honored by the presence of a new student, Gabriel. This lovely man is my husband. For many years, he was suffering from asthma. It is with great relief that I am announcing that my husband can breathe again and yoga is responsible for this cure."

The students applauded. They came to congratulate me, forming a joyous circle. Little did they know that the true healer of my afflicted lungs was a Chinese masseuse whose hands could awake the dead.

Signs of Life

After an eight-hour excision of a neoplasm on a lumbar vertebra of an adolescent girl, I traipsed in my office and poured myself a tumbler of Jack Daniel's. I closed my eyes, welcoming the dark after hours under the white incandescent lights of the operatory. But, I couldn't find stillness. I was thinking of Mantuo Luo. I repeated motivational lines extracted from inspirational books, polysyllabic mantras, chants that quiet the restless soul, but nothing worked. So I recalled aphorisms I had collected, quotes gleaned from the great thinkers.

Everything that inconveniences us allows us to define ourselves, without indispositions, no identity. It is by suffering only that one ceases to be a marionette. Space separates one skin from another. A lot of nonsense, frankly.

I turned on the news channel on the office TV. It was *Breaking News*. The reporter, a woman inappropriately dressed to deliver the news, was visibly and personally affected. The mechanized robot trotting on the volcanic surface of Io, a moon of Jupiter, had detected signs of fossil life. They were methane-based bacterial organisms. This scientific news refuted all the sacred constructs which maintain our exclusivity on earth. In the universe, no climactic act of creation, no chosen people, species, simply spontaneous cells scattered across interstellar space. The DNA of the bacteria from satellite Io were identical to earth's organisms. DNA was everywhere and the same. This is a DNA-drenched universe.

The Scent of Defeat

Just outside my office window, a crew of workers gathered. They ripped the asphalt, unearthing cables, exposing steam pipes. I called the New York City noise pollution office. An employee with a Brooklyn accent registered my grievance and promised to send an inspector to investigate. A backhoe had joined the party. Heavy equipment machinery was gathering around the site. The diesel engine of the excavator spewed smoke like a nervous volcano about to erupt. A FedEx messenger in uniform barged into my office and handed me a box.

My fingers ripped the cardboard, exposing a white feminine undergarment.

An evocative scent emanated from the intimate apparel. It was complex and difficult to name. As I was bringing the delicate lingerie closer to my face, the aroma radiated from the diaphanous material. The sender didn't write a note. Mantuo Luo was conveying her intentions through scent like bees and ants. I was determined to identify that perfume, its vocabulary, its grammar.

Although I was bone-weary from performing manually precise maneuvers in tiny spaces inside my patient's skeletal architecture for many hours, I mobilized my waning stamina. I visited fragrance stores on Fifth Avenue and engaged in exploratory conversations with salesgirls. They blushed when I produced the undergarment. They were intrigued and excited. They were eager to identify that perfume. But they couldn't. They wanted me to leave a piece of the lingerie. They'd talk to their friends in the perfume business. They brought scissors and began mutilating the scented cloth. This mystery bouquet didn't originate from the design teams of Coco Chanel, Sonia Rykiel, Paco Rabanne, Lancome, Armani, Versace, etc. Next on my agenda, I'd visit that notorious laboratory in Manhattan, the birthplace of many best-selling perfumes. I was heading toward the exit when I spotted a perfume booth with the sign of Guerlain.

The saleslady smiled.

"Yes, it's Chamade!" she whispered.

"Chamade. It's a French word."

"*'Drumbeat of a besieged city to indicate its capitulation. Wear that fragrance for the man you love, and he will know you are ready to surrender'*—that's what the label says."

"What are the ingredients?" I asked.

"Turkish rose, jasmine, lilac, black currant, hyacinth, cassis, galbanum, sandalwood, vetiver, vanilla, ambergris, and the most important and Raymond Gerlain's favorite, lily of the valley. Mr. Guerlain designed this perfume right before his death," the salesgirl told me.

Did Guerlain name that perfume because of his predicament, the proximity of his death? Was Chamade an announcement of my lover's submission to her paramour or her capitulation to her approaching extinction? Was Mantuo Luo proclaiming her abdication to my desire, or like the muezzin call, was she exhorting me to accept my annihilation?

The lily of the valley was the flower of Mary. It was known as Mary's tears, springing from her during crucifixion. Immersed in thought, I wandered down Fifth Avenue, my spirit in an incandescent state.

Toward the Waterfall

We didn't speak. Her lubricated fingers played Bach's cantata on my skin like the fingers of a virtuoso on a keyboard, exploring cutaneous regions untouched before. Her itinerary on my body map had a destination. The tide ebbed against the breakers of guilt pulverizing the petrified conscience, washing the shoreline with sparkling waves.

My life before her had been a mosaic of schedules and agendas. I had lived life in the shallows for too long. I was attracted now by the deep end of the ocean where the wrecks slept.

Her gaze was placid. She wore no jewelry. It would have distracted from her inherent luminosity. She flaunted no accessories, no accoutrements.

"I dream of you," she murmured in English.

She'd been studying English. I was glad about it. From now on, we'll talk, negotiate emotions, solve riddles. We'll not be strangers. I'll find out about her Oriental soul. She'll explore mine. Words will be the portals through which I'd travel her hidden past. I felt like a child staring at the windows of an old curiosity shop full of memorabilia and exotic toys.

Months passed. She had registered for night classes, listening to language tapes, watching tons of American movies. Her green notebook stored columns and lists of nouns, verbs, adjectives, and adverbs. Her English by now was conversational, and we could venture discussing all kinds of things with fluency.

She told me stories. One afternoon, her dad was telling the tale of the Chinese mariner who invented the compass. She was eight years old. Knocks on the door. Students of the Red Guard crashed into her apartment and broke through her father's library, where he had amassed his collections. They were chanting slogans. They seized all his books and threw them from their sixth-floor window. Family photo albums joined the books into the pile in the courtyard. Kerosene was poured. Fires were lit. Her father's treasure, gathered from many years of scientific expeditions, burned through the night. Forty years of accumulated riches lovingly preserved were cremated that afternoon. The district leader demoted her father from his position as a professor of herbal medicine at the university. He was assigned latrine duties in the building of public transportation. Her eyes moistened as she described her father's humiliation. He was never the same after this. He found solace in plum wine and died few years later of a heart attack while taking a shower.

After a long silence, tears again welled up in her eyes.

"I miss my dog," she moaned.

"What was his name?"

"Zhengzhong—it means 'loyal.' He was my best friend. One day, he disappeared. I look for him everywhere, talk to the neighbors, the police, the district boss. One afternoon, I hear him barking in the courtyard. Five men boil water in a big pot. They tie Zhengzhong legs. They were going to cook him. My dog was calling me. I yelled at the men, 'He is my dog! Leave him alone!' I could see my dog was looking at me, begging for help. 'I will report you to the district boss!' I screamed. They yelled back, 'We're hungry! We are sorry!' They cut his neck, cut him in pieces, and boiled them."

That was the aftermath of the Great Famine instituted by Mao himself. How hungry they were in the provinces, millions and millions of men, women, and children in the most agricultural nation in the world.

She turned to me, grasping my hand.

One day, I caught her leafing through a paperback with Chinese characters.

"It is a poem by Mo Shang Sang," she said.

"You read poetry?"

"I write poetry when I was a child. Revolution people burned my notebooks. I see fire eat my poems," she said, a tremor in her voice.

She embraced me.

"I will write poems in English. It will be easier because it is not my language," she said, pressing her vanilla-scented lips against my neck.

"Yes, write in English," I urged.

"I have learned five new English words every day, for many days. Every week I learned thirty-five new words. I will speak like a lady," she said, submitting her mouth to my tongue.

She undressed, removing her blouse, unzipping her skirt. Fashionably, she was stuck in the fifties, an age that appreciated stockings and garter belts.

"I remember by heart every poem I have written. One day I will translate them for you," she said.

She remained half-dressed, half-undressed, letting me contemplate her skin.

"Your body is poetry to me," I whispered.

She stretched, melting her body against mine like two alloys commingling into a new metal, the result of a flawless fusion.

The tableau of my counterfeit existence had deteriorated. I had yearned for her my whole life, and I didn't know it, distracted myself with obligations and appearance to elude my thirst. I knew every hour without her had been squandered. My past pretensions, my future aspirations had been a blur. Only with her could I reinvent the present.

*****

"Damn it!" Maren yelled, filled with an urge to destroy the man she had loved.

*****

Her telephone numbers acquired magical powers. I became fascinated by the plurality of eights. They were four eights. Eight stands for infinity. I cherished the symbolism of that numerology. I was elated by this coincidence and delighted in its implications.

A sense of inevitability prevailed. A few days later, I visited her again. I needed to loot her. We melted ores in the pit of our organs, forging sensations that could withstand oppressive cravings in the furnace of our hearts. In this ravenous cauldron of our hunger, we glowed, bathed in brightness, like asteroids in that moment when they come down screaming, inflamed in the atmosphere.

She handed me a blue envelope. Inside a card, she had written a sentence in English.

It read, "*Forgive my amphibian heart.*"

It was a one-line poem of great beauty, of untold possibilities. It turned me on in an incomprehensible way. I didn't understand it, but it filled my mind with images of the sea.

The Heart

We rendezvoused at Tuscany, a Northern Italian restaurant.

I had arrived before the appointed time and occupied a booth. I ordered a glass of Bianco di Pitigliano and distracted myself by reading news from China.

She sashayed into the room in a tight-fitting persimmon-red dress. The gilded spike heels of her shoes, like the twin tails of a golden dragon, scratched the floor tiles.

Her walk was languorous, as if she were moving against some inherent inertia, forcing the thrust of her thighs and the swing of her shoulders against some invisible resistance. She looked like an actress impersonating a submissive captive.

For a moment, I felt like an absolute beginner, awkward and terrified.

She planted a kiss on my frozen lips. Her face glowed like a lantern in the Festival of the New Moon. A white powder with magenta hues adorned her cheeks. Lipstick the color of pomegranate highlighted her lips. Her dark eyes absorbed all the lights from the chandelier.

"Would you like a glass of wine?" I asked.

"Cranberry juice."

I stared at her august face. Words Richard Burton wrote after having met the nineteen-year-old Elizabeth Taylor I had stored in my cell phone. I read his words out loud:

> *She was extraordinarily beautiful that I nearly laughed out loud. She was famine, fire, destruction, and plague. Her breasts were apocalyptic; they would topple empires before they withered... Her body was*

a miracle of construction. She was unquestionably gorgeous. She was lavish. She was a dark unyielding largesse. She was, in short, too bloody much... Those violet-blue eyes had an odd glint. Eons passed, civilizations came and went, while these cosmic headlights examined my flawed personality. Every pockmark on my face became a crater of the moon.

"Thank you," she murmured, her voice suffused with emotions.

The cranberry arrived.

"It is a beautiful color," she said.

Her lips parted. She sipped the fuchsia liquid.

The waiter approached. I ordered a seafood entrée, calamari Florentine style for both of us.

Cautiously, she bit into the mollusk, savoring the subtle sauce. I was staring at her white teeth lacerating the sliced squid. She didn't want any dessert. After dinner, we drove to her apartment in Flushing, Queens.

We walked down a street bordered by maple trees in full foliage. It was a drab utilitarian apartment building on Union Street in Flushing, the abode of Chinese, Korean, and Japanese blue-collar workers. The edifice smelled of sweet and sour spices, and the walls showed sign of wear and tear, the results of many years of neglect. We took the elevator to the fifth floor, and at the end of a long, dingy corridor, she unlocked the door to unit 5E.

It was a studio apartment that served as living quarters and storage room to two girls. A handmade wooden bunk bed leaned against a beige wall. There were boxes and valises stacked up against a wall. A climate of poverty and desolation reigned. A girl in the kitchen was boiling tea. The teakettle screamed. The roommate approached me. She was limping. She said few words and bowed. Mantuo Luo translated.

"Oolong tea."

"Sure," I said.

"She is my roommate. Her husband beat her in China. He pushed her down the stairs. She breaks her hip. She ran away. Came to America. Her name is Ju. It is *chrysanthemum*."

"Where is your bed?" I asked.

"This one." She pointed at the upper one. "Ju cannot climb ladder."

The roommate brought a steaming mug. The tea was scalding. I inhaled the aroma, which was vivifying.

"Ju cannot get a job. Restaurant bosses don't want to hire her because of her leg. Not even in the kitchen. She is my friend. I pay rent for her."

"I can get her a job at the hospital in the laundry room. It's a difficult job, but the money is good," I said.

"Can I tell her?"

"Of course."

Ju's eyes lit up. She grabbed my hand and kissed it.

"You're the god of mercy, Gabriel."

She became quiet, introverted.

"I'm sorry you see where I live," she moaned.

A hard silence followed. I was stricken by the poverty of the place, the despair in the air. I could help this woman I loved.

A Sudden Serenity

The Dutch settled in Flushing in 1628 by purchasing land from the Matinecock Indians. Peter Stuyvesant, the Dutch governor of Manhattan, persecuted Quakers who escaped his tyranny by settling in Flushing. In the early 1800s, a group of African Americans, drawn by the tolerance of the Quakers, settled there. By the middle of the twentieth century, Chinese, Koreans, Japanese, Filipinos, and Hindus arrived in Flushing, bringing their culinary and musical traditions to Queens, New York.

Mantuo Luo moved into a one-bedroom apartment on Cherry Avenue in Flushing. She went shopping for furniture and bought a king-size mahogany bed, a pine dining room table with four wicker chairs made in Thailand, an avocado-green sofa made in Malaysia, a fuchsia-colored armchair, two Belgian-made replicas of Persian carpets with Khorasan and Tabriz designs, lots of kitchen things, and chromed bed lamps and brass torchères with dimmers.

When I arrived in the apartment that afternoon, Mantuo was sleeping.

"I'd love a bath," she moaned.

Steam rose from the tub like foam from a heated cauldron in a cloth-dye workshop.

She entered the bathroom, the bedsheet covering her body.

"I like it very hot," she whimpered.

I set to work scrubbing her back.

"Be careful with my neck."

She raised her leg in a cataract of foam. I responded to the invitation, sliding my fingers into the dark knot shimmering ghostlike under the opaque water. My insistent hand soaped her protruding flesh, grinding the soft mound. She bucked, emitting a tiny whine.

She grabbed my slackening fingers and continued the scouring. She was riding a wave turning into a tide.

She emerged from the tub, letting the waters fall out of her glistening skin. I wrapped her body with a terry-cloth towel.

"I'm tired," she murmured languidly.

She stretched on the bed and quickly faded into the fog of sleep.

I sat on the armchair by the window, contemplating her radiant flesh. My hand moved, repeatedly stroking, extracting joy from the moistened valve. I pushed away the comforter, exposing her dark angularity. In a succession of spasms, I spilled on that geography. I seized her limp hand and kissed it with a reverence that bordered on piety.

I sat on the armchair to watch that relic lying sumptuously against a propped pillow. Time passed. I had to leave. I bowed in adoration, kowtowing like a courtier taking leave from an Asiatic potentate. I slithered out of the room like a submissive attendant exiting a royal court chamber.

I reflected on my ceremonial departure, which belonged to a world long vanished. I reminisced about my mother. I adored her once. I was six years old. That kind of reverence I could trace to those early years when my veneration for my mother reached its apex. What is the hankering that draws us toward our mother? What is that devotion for that shrine we have been forever banished from? Doesn't life begin outside that portal? But is there any possibility of beatitude away from that temple where we were conceived? Have I found a substitute for that original chapel one can never repossess? Have I transformed a taboo into a field of splendor?

Arson

Alvard dropped in my office unannounced. He arrived looking like a man just risen from a fever. He sat across me at the chair reserved for patients in consultation.

"Are you still seeing her?" he asked.

"Yes."

"She doesn't return my calls. When did you see her last?"

"I had an appointment last week," I said.

"How was she?"

"She's fine."

"Do you talk about me?"

"Never."

"Does she bring me up?"

"No."

"I thought you stopped seeing her."

"I tried."

"She's never stood me up before. Is she ill?"

"Not that I know."

He was ill-equipped to deal with the rejection. Things were falling apart. The center couldn't hold. I had never asked Mantuo Luo to stop ministering to my friend. But she knew I wished it and was distancing herself from him.

He looked like a man without a compass. His eyes fixed mine.

"You're a strange fish," he said, then he walked away.

I was disturbed by Alvard's visit. His lust was unattended. My mind evoked that absurd paradox. Why must the life of our species be preserved and our cravings satisfied by means of organs we use several times a day as a drain for impurities? I had read, as a student in anatomy class, that Leonardo da Vinci, against the orders of the

Inquisition that forbade dissection of bodies, examined the internal morphology of criminals. He drew scrupulously musculature and skeleton, arteries and nerves, yet in his meticulous drawings, he made an error which stunned scholars and critiques. He charted two channels in the male genital area: the urethra for the passage of urine and another for the transmission of sperm. He couldn't accept that nature would have one conduit for both functions, excremental and reproductive. God wouldn't combine both events. How could the sacred and the bestial commingle in one path? His mind drew a different model where he separated both functions. Didn't Saint Augustine, a frequent visitor of brothels in his youth, newly converted, write "*inter faeces et urinem nascimur*" (between feces and urine we are born)? I recalled a joke that Robin Williams made in one of his stand-up gig. He asked, "Why did God build an entertainment complex in the vicinity of a dump site?"

Voyagers

We lined up, interstellar travelers outside the portal to the immense bubble, the planetarium, two earthlings about to enter an alien sphere for a planetary journey. The dome lit up with a myriad of stars. The narrator announced the subject of the documentary: *"When Galaxies Collide."*

The universe is expanding at vertiginous speeds, and bodies are moving away from each other. Cosmic crashes occur because the gravitational forces of galaxies attract them to each other. With their thousands of stars, they smash against each other in a pyrotechnic display, a celebration of a billion Fourth of July and Bastille Day captured by the Hubble telescope and projected on the concave screen of the planetarium.

"I'd like to go there," Mantuo Luo murmured, craning her swanlike neck, gazing at the firmament, pointing with a slender finger at some location in the galaxy.

Stargazers

I hauled in the large cardboard box and two folding chairs. The scent of Chinese sauces filled the air. She had labored the whole day to prepare dinner.

"What is it?" she asked, caressing the humongous box.

She unwrapped the package, exposing a long black cylinder and a tripod.

There was nobody on the roof this late at night. We mounted the telescope, connected the wires, and turned on devices.

I read out loud the document of purchase from the Astronomical Society.

"Congratulations. Now you are the proud owner of star Y603402 in the Swan galaxy. It's registered under your name, Mantuo Luo. It's yours forever. The telescope has a minicomputer with a star positioning system that can locate any star. Press the coordinates into this keyboard, the star code."

The telescope gyrated and then stopped. It targeted a particular region of the galaxy. Lenses adjusted themselves to capture the feeble source of light. Mantuo approached the viewfinder. Her eyes widened.

"Look, we can look at the star magnified on the television screen," I said.

I turned on the screen. The opalescent light glowed with mineral life radiating a wide halo. The star gleamed, projecting yellow flares.

"It's beautiful," Mantuo beamed.

We sat on chairs, holding hands, transfixed by that vision.

Stars are not enjoying the same popularity they once had. As long as it was believed that one's fate was determined by these astral bodies, they were feared and revered. As children, we thought they were bulbs lit up by God in the night sky to illuminate us. We believed they winked at us. Now, we know they're blind and helpless rocks captured by magnetic fields, hostages of bigger rocks. They are a constant and brutal intimation of our insignificance. They remind us we are specks in a field of bigger specks. TV astronomers are agents of doom. There are as many astronomers as there are preachers. They predict an approaching collision. The word *disaster* is etymologically intriguing? It is made of *dis*, which means "evil," and *aster*, which means "star": evil star. This word entered our everyday parlance while hiding its macabre origin. Velikovski exposed a universe in turmoil. *Worlds in Collision* hit the scientific establishment like a Molotov cocktail. Based on research in the mythological texts of ancient civilizations and revelations in geology and racial psychoanalysis, this Russian Jew announced that earth was once ravaged by the tail of a passing comet around 1500 BC. The author, who was a trained psychoanalyst and a friend of Freud, believes this trauma was experienced by human survivors who repressed that cataclysmal memory. Academia laughed at this catastrophic vision, but after they launched sophisticated research satellites with telescopes, this scientist was validated. The universe is in convulsion, destruction, and re-creation. We are the passengers of this spaceship navigating through spaces littered with mineral wrecks vestiges of the astronomical carnage.

Blissful Geometry

In the weeks that followed, Mantuo Luo had given me her sublime body with complete abandon. In our lovemaking, I soared. She didn't. She explained that Chinese tradition forbade the auditory manifestation of physical pleasure. An unassuming stance and detachment were the norms during sexual commingling. Among Chinese women, the site of pleasure was a place of uncleanliness. I professed I revered her anatomy which was a living gallery featuring many objets d'art, sculptures of infinite shapes and textures, protuberances of exquisite designs. Her sex evoked culinary words that qualify taste: "acidity," "astringency," "cayenne," "piquancy," "papaya flesh," "pungency," "the scent of pears and persimmons," "coriander and turmeric," "steamed vegetable dumplings and other unnamed flavors like the shore tide," "the mineral taste of waves and sea boulders," "the velvety taste of oysters," etc.

Her view of sex was startling. Mao Zedong's fake puritanism had damaged her. I didn't tell her what I had read about his sexual proclivities, that he would send agents to the military schools for girls to select the most attractive ones to bring to his bed.

"Mother warned me about beauty. It confuses men. My face will dishonor our family, she said. Feng, our neighbor's son, was a bad boy. Feng's mother had important position in a local Communist committee. When I was fifteen years old, I threw Feng's love poems in the garbage. He was with Revolutionary Guards. My parents forced me to marry him. I cried for many days. I ask my father to help me. My father was a puppet. He was very shy.

"Mantuo Luo never forgave her father's complicity with her mother, his policies of appeasement and conciliation, his uselessness in time of crisis. Duty, family obligations, honor, saving face prevailed. The ghosts of Confucius and Mao Zedong ruled this household. Unable to chart her own destiny, she surrendered to a fate of abject obedience in matters of the heart. She married her neighbor's son, the student who organized the raid against her home, the destroyer of her father's library, the incinerator of all the family photos, the arsonist of her poetry.

"I hated my husband. He complained to my mother that I was not a wife. One night, he was drunk. He hit me many times. He forced me many nights. I was throwing up in the morning. My son was born, but I couldn't love him. I gave him to my mother. When he was eight years old, I came to America."

In that moment, I thought of Liriope, the water nymph who was ravaged by the river god.

I thought of her son, Narcissus, who grew up motherless. I thought of Mantuo's son abandoned by his mother, raised by her mother.

Narcissus

It's strange how myths illustrate human upheavals. We live in a narcissistic age. Many men are called narcissistic.

The water nymph Liriope was playing on the shore of a river when the river god, Cephissus, saw her. She rebuked his advances, so he assaulted her. She was pregnant. When the boy Narcissus was born, she abandoned him because she never wanted him. Motherless, he raised himself, and when he became an adolescent, he would spend days looking at the surface of the water, looking for his mother, a water nymph. The pond offered only the reflection of his face.

He was turned into a flower, narcissus, which, when eaten, can induce sleep. From the name of that flower, we have the word *narcotics*.

The Sky Travelers

I was armed with two bottles of Veuve Clicquot. I hoped other memories would surface with the help of alcohol, which is a soul lubricant. We climbed to the roof of her building and bracketed the telescope to that region of the galaxy where she reigned. We located her star and toasted to the continuity of its brilliance. We drank, commemorating Mantu Luo's place in the firmament.

"May it shine over us here on Earth and bring light to the darkness in our lives," I said.

We identified the Andromeda galaxy, our cosmic neighbor, which, in one hundred million years, will collide with our Milky Way.

I uncorked the next bottle. I looked into her eyes. They reflected the speckled sky.

"Tell me about your father," I asked.

"My father cleaned bathrooms at the Department of Transportation. After, they send him to re-education camp to learn Maoist doctrine. My mother received a permit to go see him in the camp. My mother didn't know why she receives permit. Nobody goes to camp to see family member. The camp was full of smart people. Father sleeps in a wood bed without mattress. The camp boss didn't like my father because he read too many books. My father looked like a dead man because they didn't give him much food. Father was eating the scallion cakes Mother made in our kitchen. The camp boss, Lien Sheu, talked to my mother. He looked at me like a snake looks at a mouse. Back to our house, Mother can't fall asleep on her mattress because my father lies on wood bed. Mother writes many letters to party members about my father. He is a good man, a party member in the war against the nationalists. He walks on foot with the Red Army to Shangsi Province during the Long March. Many weeks we received letters from my father. My mother couldn't believe because you never receive letters. 'I want to read the letters,' I say. She yells at me like a madwoman. I hid in the bathroom. I was afraid she was going to hurt me. She never talks about the letters again. One morning, after Mother goes to work at the tractor factory, I clean the house. I turn over the mattress. I find the letters.

"Lien Sheu wanted me to work in his kitchen. I could learn cooking, he said. Lien Sheu said he gives more food to my father if my mother sends her daughter. In the letter, Father tells Mother to do what Lien Sheu wants. Mother understood that Lien Sheu wanted me because I was a virgin. She was disgusted at Father, who was selling his daughter. I write a letter to Lien Sheu. Weeks passed. Winter came. The winds from Manchuria bring snow. One morning in the classroom, two soldiers come. The car is government car, black and shiny. The driver was a sweet young man. He drives far in the mountains. It is a beautiful house. I sit in the living room. A big photo of Mao is on the wall. He looks like a fat… How you call it? Frog. I am a fly. I am afraid the long tongue comes out from his mouth and he swallows me. I hear water in another room. Lien Sheu calls my name. I go to the bathroom. Lien Sheu was in the tub. He looks like a big shrimp in the water. He had no hair on his head, and his mouth was like the mouth of Xun," she picked up her smartphone and activated the translation app, "sturgeon—it's a fish. 'Wash my back,' he says. 'Father is hungry,' I said. 'Rice is for the army,' he says. 'I don't want to be an orphan,' I cry. 'My jujube, Mao, our father will look after him,' he said.

"'I only have one father,' I say. 'I can arrest you for speaking ugly about the father of our country.' I wanted to drown him. 'Your beauty, my longam, makes me forget I am old and dying.' He throws water on my face. 'Do you like perfume? Take that box, open it. French perfume. It belongs to my wife. Keep it. How old are you, twelve? Do you have woman's blood yet? You are a courageous girl, and you will help your father. Get me my cigarettes. They're in the living room, on my desk,' he says. He gives me a cigarette. 'American. Very good!' he says.

"His body is the color of pavement. His sex looks like the head of a pond turtle. 'I'm hungry.' He grabs my arm and pulls me to the dining room. Many dishes on the table. 'Do you like duo jiao yutou?' he asked. 'No.' 'You like hong wei yuchi?' He eats a roasted shark fin. He drinks a lot of sorghum wine. 'Get undressed!' he yells. 'I am a virgin.' 'Take off your dress, stupid girl!' he yells. 'You look like a squid,' I say. He presses my face against a dish full of crabs. Hot chili sauce hurts my eyes, they burn. He goes under my dress with his fingers. I am a clam, and he is an octopus. The ginger and pepper sauce in his fingers make fire inside. 'You are crabmeat!' he yells. He puts his mouth down there and licks me. I take a big crab leg and hit him in the head. He yells very loud. There's blood on his face. His car driver comes running. I thought he was going to kill me. He says, 'I'm sorry.' He takes me to the car. I never told my mother what happened. But few years later, Lien Sheu was smoking an American cigarette in a balcony on the thirty-third floor of the Center for Agriculture in Tien Jin. It was his last cigarette."

"What happened?" I asked.

"It's my secret," she muttered.

The air that separated us evaporated.

She raised her ether face toward the night sky, taking in the intermittent lights. Millions of miles from the rooftop of that apartment building in Flushing, in the pedestrian borough of Queens, galaxies, aflame with primordial fury, were colliding madly at the edge of the heartless universe.

She killed the guy! I reflected.

The night regained an eerie quiescence.

She grabbed my hand and guided it to her breasts. With incomprehensible frenzy, she made me claw at her nipples, lacerating the thin skin until I drew blood. She forced my blood-soaked fingers in her mouth and began sucking them with relish. She applied her dank tongue to my lips, flooding me with her saliva and blood. She ripped her undergarment and began foraging inside her sex, luring my fingers to join in her internal exploration. The viscous mixture with abundant menstrual blood flowed through my hand. A chorus of sighs and howls reverberated from her windpipe. She directed my head, cramming my mouth against her sex. Her caustic brine scalded my tongue. She tasted ferrous and coppery. I endured the pain, drowning in a sinkhole. The taste of chalk and rotten pineapples infected my sinuses. No disinfectant could mask the stench. The acids in my stomach were edging their way up in the back of my throat. A fat moth with bluish wings collided and crashed against my forehead. My bruised larynx wanted to scream. I could only produce a gargling sound. I tore myself from her embrace and left the roof of her building, staggering down the staircase to the shelter of my car.

*****

Maren pressed the Pause button. Her temples were pounding. She removed and pocketed the USB drive and drove home. It was a strenuous journey to her hideaway in Rye.

She staggered through the dark foyer and crouched on the stairs. The din in her head took on a sickening rhythm, like the rotors of a helicopter. She choked the yell with her tongue sealing its eruption. She was sweating a flood. The smell of rotten fruits choked the olfactory cells of her nasal cavern. She had absorbed her husband's narrative in all its sensorial decay.

She shut her eyes, her ears, longing to recapture that inner silence that had degenerated into an uproar. To attenuate the internal vortex would be an achievement worthy of her spirit. All these years, her disciplined body had achieved a serenity through the systematic practice of yoga. She was facing a turbulence of great magnitude. She visualized her body illuminated by a single candle, performing asanas. With meticulous precision, her muscles executed the poses. She had accomplished her objective: detachment. Nothing she had read affected her senses. She was immune to the tribulations of the diary, the vicissitudes of her married life. Her transcendence was a blessed state of disunion with the world. She had escaped the coordinates of her personal presence in the world. She welcomed this state of apartness and let it linger. After a while, she opened her eyes. Curiosity was gnawing. She wanted to know. She barged into her husband's study and inserted the gadget in his laptop. But she didn't press the Enter button yet. She turned on the FM radio. A symphony by Haydn filled the room. Soothed by the music, she savored the lull.

Devastation

I played back in my mind the events of the evening to find signs I had missed, traces that could guide me to an understanding. She had described her maltreatment using imagery from that print of Hokusai's *The Dream of the Fisherman's Wife*, which adorned a wall in her massage chamber. Lien Sheu, she'd said, was penetrating her like an octopus perforating a clam. I'd ordered a plate of calamari at the Italian restaurant. Were these associations with crustaceans a coincidence? Did she dramatize that encounter with the camp boss to stir in me infinite revulsion, compassion? She orchestrated that raid on her nipple and her sex forcing my fingers to do the plunder, my mouth to sack her organ. Exquisite rapture she experienced in that devastation. I'd become a sex toy for her masochistic thrills? Orgasm was achieved in the pinnacle of pain? Was that organ invasion by Lien Sheu as repulsive as she described it, or was it a moment of harrowing delectation? Under the canopy of the galaxies, with star Y603402 overlooking us, that night was ruined by the introduction of horror into our Eden.

Sea Life

She wasn't in the apartment when I arrived. A school of baby octopuses were swimming in the kitchen sink. What was this fascination with crustaceans?

Sound of keys in the lock. Mantuo Luo came in with yellow plastic bags full of groceries.

"I'm sorry, honey."

"There are octopuses in the sink," I protested.

"Go lie down. I'll wake you up when it's ready."

I ambled to the bedroom and lay down. My cock was aching. I staggered to the kitchen, grabbed her neck, lowered her skirt, and plunged. Baby octopuses were crawling up her arms. With blind enthusiasm, I stabbed the secret aperture. Her body bucked. Her other muscle, shocked at the sudden violation, tightened its grip. It wrapped around, trapping the intruder.

I was panting, exhausted.

I was thirsty. I opened the liebfraumilch.

I sat on the dining room table chair.

The room filled with the scents of ginger, coriander, scallion, and soy sauce.

"Open your mouth," she murmured in my ear, feeding me a sliced tentacle gleaming in red brine.

"I don't want you to do massage to strangers," I said.

Rival

I was updating my medical charts in my office when Alvard burst in.

"She's not there anymore," he sobbed.

"What're you talking about?"

"She doesn't work there anymore. Have you been seeing her lately?"

"I haven't seen her for weeks?"

A knot was tightening in my stomach.

"So, you're done with her?" he panted.

"My asthma is a thing of the past," I said, confidently.

His eyes had lost their luster. They were as colorless as water.

"I've got to locate her," he said.

"You're in love?"

"I don't know," he said, rubbing his forehead the color of gray slate.

"She doesn't answer my calls," he said, hanging his head.

"Maybe she got busted," I offered.

"What do you mean?"

"She's an undocumented alien. There's a chance they deported her."

"It takes months to deport someone. I've got to find out what happened. You're gonna help?"

"Sure."

"If she calls, you let me know?"

"Of course."

"You know, I think I never knew her," he said in a confessional tone.

"Why do you say that?"

"I don't know," he rambled.

His gaze turned inward, catching a thought he couldn't articulate. He shuddered as if too close to some truth his mind couldn't conjure, his words couldn't name.

"You've created a fantasy world, and look at you! You've built a palace, Gabriel, a castle in the clouds packed with electricity. They're going to detonate, you know. Can't you hear the distant thunder?" he stuttered.

He managed to stand up, his muscles exerting themselves against gravity.

"The thought that you could be my rival?" he grieved, a deep sadness on his unshaven face.

He looked at the room, examining the walls, concentrating on the ceiling.

"Do you see it?" he asked, suddenly alarmed.

"What?" I asked.

"There! A shadow. It's moving."

He was hallucinating.

"He's come for us, Gabriel. Are your affairs in order?"

He left my office like a reflection wishing to be a man.

Our present consciousness is not equipped to deal with the termination of things. In *The Denial of Death*, Ernest Becker proposes that every ideological system is an attempt to deny the irrevocable and offer a refutation for our disappearance, an ersatz of immortality.

Alvard had lost Mantuo, who anchored his soul. I was responsible for the rift. What transformation had taken place within me that had designed an alter ego capable of betraying the laws of friendship?

Do we always know the motives for our transgressions? Mantuo Luo trespassed into a region of the self I had never ventured in.

Island

Fire Island, New York was our destination. I remembered to take my sunglasses on this excursion. Although it was September and the luminosity was attenuated, my eyes had developed a sensitivity to light.

The Great South Bay shimmered under the diffuse morning light. The ferryboat docked at the Ocean Beach hamlet.

There were no cars in the island, no buses. We ambled on a wooden-plank path toward the beach escorted by maritime pines. Pastel-colored bungalows dotted the arboreal landscape. Stillness was all around us, a serenity unmarred by woodpeckers or Con Edison bulldozers. The beach embraced us with saffron sand and billowing waves. We unfolded our beach chairs and opened our beach umbrellas. We sipped champagne. I dozed off. Time streamed unmeasured. When I woke up, Mantuo Luo wasn't there. Families and couples had colonized the strand. Children were splashing among waves. A golden retriever was pursuing a poodle, begging for romance.

In the distance, a woman was prospecting the sand. It was Mantuo Luo. I joined her.

"My father collected seagrasses."

She had gathered algae, blue leaves the tide had spit out. Near the waterline, a teenager had molded in sand the body of a woman. The statue lay on her back, her breasts like mosques cupolas. Her thighs were full and her belly tantalizing. Her vulva was realistic, detailed, and opened like a canna lily. Will this Pygmalion ravish his silica Galatea? Like colored sand mandalas executed with infinite devotion by Tibetan monks, the sand woman was constructed to be annihilated? A wave washed over her brittle body, crushing her pudenda, melting her pointed nipples, ending any hope for a transient affair.

Disemboweled, this mineral Venus offered her hollowed-out carcass. The sculptor, enraged at her impermanence, kicked her frittered remains, and ambled away, casting a despondent look at her decaying chest.

We returned to our corner of the beach, listening to the rhythm of the tide, inhaling the sea wind, watching the waves inching their way up toward our enclosure. Under the afternoon sun, her skin was a tinted indigo hue. I expected to see fins sprout from her abdomen. There was a taste of copper pennies in my mouth. I was thirsty.

"Can I get you anything?"

"Coffee."

I walked to town. At the grocery store, I gulped a quart of orange juice. I picked up two cups of coffee. When I reached Mantuo, she was on a call.

"My brother is a spice store merchant in Tien Jin. He buys American herbs we don't have in China."

A large cumulus moved away, exposing the ardent sun. The solar beams strafed the sand.

"Did you hear?" she asked.

"No."

"The waves, they're calling me," she announced, sprinting toward the waves.

The sun was oppressive. I covered my chest with the towel. I closed my eyes and nodded off.

Somebody was yelling. I woke up. The lifeguard emergency truck was speeding toward a crowd. A police officer was applying resuscitation techniques on a lifeless bather. The lifeguard massaged and pressured her chest briskly. Spasms wracked her torso as she regurgitated seawater. Shivering, she coughed violently. I stood there listless, disengaged.

Mantuo Luo refused to be driven to the hospital. She resisted the lifeguards' recommendations. The police insisted. At the hospital, her immigration status would be exposed. I flashed my hospital medical ID.

I dried her drenched body and wrapped it in a towel. We sat in the sand for a while to let her rest.

"What happened?" I asked.

"My mother was a swimming coach. She never taught me how to swim."

Her gaze mourned an ancient loss.

We sat on the upper deck of the ferry. The sea air filled us with scents of suntan lotion and oleander flowers.

I was a ferry shuttling between the harbor of conventions and the shores of profligacy. I'd jettisoned my anchor and had never retrieved it. Rudderless, I was sailing my barge, letting the current guide me. What was the lure of the unknown?

Seagulls hovered over the boat. They quarreled and fought a few feet above our heads. A bird pilfered a sandwich right out of a kid's hands. Armed with a folded sun umbrella, I struck a seagull. It screeched. At that moment, I craved a shotgun. What carnage I visualized; what slaughter I craved.

Chemical Heart

Was my infatuation with Mantuo Luo due to chemical changes? I loved her because she healed me of my asthma, my cynicism, my fatalism. Did her private scents stir the infant's repressed memories of maternal fragrances of an intimate nature?

The hospital auditorium was packed with physicians, nurses, social workers, etc. In the last row of the orchestra, I spotted Alvard.

The topic of the lecture was *The Chemistry of Love* by Dr. Sonia Berg, the reigning neuropharmacologist en vogue in mental health circles.

Dr. Sonia Berg was an anorectic woman with hair in a chignon and intellectual glasses. She could be a poster girl for an eyewear company for the elderly crowd. She approached the plexiglass lectern.

"Have you been in love? Your brain is susceptible to chemical permutations. It is chemistry that dictates passion, craving, erotic dalliances. Was Mark Anthony's adoration for Cleopatra triggered by chemical reactions in his Italian brain? Many years ago, Freud said anatomy is destiny. I propose chemistry is destiny. I have invited a patient I have treated chemically for a love obsession. I would like to introduce you to Whitney."

A college age girl ambled in and sat on a blue armchair at the center of the stage. She looked amorphous, resigned to being in the spotlight, exposed to the invasive gaze and inquisitive minds of a horde of mental health professionals, a guinea pig displayed after a laboratory experiment.

"Thank you for being with us, Whitney. Please tell us the emotional crisis you faced one year ago," Dr. Berg asked.

"I was having trouble keeping up with the homework in my computer science class, so the teacher recommended a tutor. Giselle was a graduate student. We would meet twice a week in the science library for our tutorial lessons. After the lesson, we'd have lunch outside campus. I found myself thinking about Giselle a lot. I was stalking her in Facebook, Instagram, and Twitter. We'd go shopping, to the movies. One time, I kissed her in the movie theater. I wanted more from the relationship. She didn't want to. I would call her twenty times a day. I'd send her tons of texts and e-mails. I was causing a lot of grief. I made an appointment with a psychoanalyst. On his couch, I talked a lot about my childhood. I was not in love with my mother. Her passion was baking the perfect Irish soda bread. I was not molested by my father, who was a fanatic bass fisherman. I never saw my parents make love, nor did I care. My brother didn't tie me up in the basement, and my neighbor, who drove me sometimes to school, didn't molest me. Few months later, I stopped going to my shrink. I read this article about brain chemistry. I called Dr. Berg."

"Thank you, Whitney. Let's look at the brain as a chemical factory. Let's start with my favorite brain neurotransmitter: dopamine. It is associated with focused attention, goal-directed behavior, that determination to own that car or get that degree or get that girl. That unstoppable drive towards the love object, that persistence in love, that heated pursuit, that compulsion to win at all costs make the dopamine cells in your brain release more dopamine. Yes, thrill, elation, ecstasy, hyperactivity, exhilaration are the results of overproductivity of dopamine. There is another brain chemical norepinephrine, which is derived from dopamine, which contributes greatly to that feeling of exaggerated exhilaration and is associated with sleeplessness, excess energy, loss of appetite, etc. Addiction rapture—in fact, all the addictions are caused by high levels of dopamine. I diagnosed Whitney with high levels of dopamine triggered by nascent feelings towards Giselle. Now how to lower Whitney's dopamine production I blamed for her mania? Researchers have discovered that higher level of serotonin reduces the amount of dopamine in the brain and causes a lowering of elation, enthusiasm, and mania. Therefore, I prescribed a daily dosage of Lexapro, which stimulates serotonin brain cells to produce more serotonin, therefore raising levels of that chemical which lowers dopamine and norepinephrine. Whitney, how did you experience the Lexapro regimen?"

"In about five days, I was noticing I was not obsessing as much about Giselle. After a week, it got much easier. I still wanted her, but it was not like an obsession anymore."

I left the lecture in a deep state of reflection. Did Mantuo Luo overstimulate my dopamine cells, producing an abundance of that chemical? My curiosity about a diagnosis for my condition kept me awake that night. The weeks that followed were spent researching psychological conditions studying all the categories in DSM5, that physical desk reference for mental illnesses.

My symptoms could lead me to many diagnoses, but it's manic-depressive, or the way they call it today, because some diagnoses are more fashionable than others, bipolar disorder, that fits me best. I had all the signs: feelings of euphoria, abnormal excitement, elevated mood, needing less sleep, feeling irritable, engaging in risky behavior such as impulsive sexual encounters, thoughts of death, depressive features. Was I experiencing manic depression, or was it a complete breakdown nonmedical people call love?

The Ides of March

I was driving home one night surfing the channels of talk radios when I dropped in a conversation between a talk show host and a woman with an accent who promoted her newly designed program to divine the future with accuracy. This necromancer's virtual name was Sybil, named after the famous diviner of Delphi. The modern augurer, the app architect, was an artificial intelligence designed by a dropout from Columbia University computer science's graduate center, a student named Padma Subramaniam. She flaunted her revolutionary algorithm, a breakthrough in the art of divination. Sybil, her design, promised, offered accurate predictions. Sybil accessed global astrological information, auspices pronounced by priests of ancient civilizations, creating an encyclopedic database. To hear omens, one must subscribe with a credit or debit card, then announce time, date, and city of birth by phone.

Sybil welcomed me to the site and presented a menu of services. For $99, she would pronounce sayings that will be directly applicable to my present life; for $199, a report of my present dilemma would be delivered; for $299, a comprehensive account of my future would be disclosed. Sybil encouraged me to design a private password. I pressed 8080, the numbers for infinity and nothingness. Intent on tricking this astrologer, I submitted an erroneous date and city of birth. She didn't correct me. I raised the ante and signed for a deluxe treatment, the $299 package. I wanted to know what she had to say about my future, for all that's worth. "What will it be?" I asked. She proposed a riddle. In it, if I could unravel it, I would I know what the stars have in store from me. I suddenly panicked and terminated the call.

"The fault, dear Brutus, is not in our stars but in ourselves, that we are underlings"—that's what Cassius said to Brutus, who wanted to assassinate Caesar. Cassius was right!

But he couldn't alter his destiny.

Lifeless

My wife was invited to attend a conference of yoga practitioners in Atlanta. I spent my nights in Mantuo Luo's apartment.

I was awakened from the valley of sleep by Mantuo Luo's heated altercation inside her dream. She woke up, left the bed. In the living room, she installed herself in the divan and wrote on a notebook. She slipped the notebook inside a drawer in her desk and returned to bed, wrapping herself with the comforter.

In the morning, I wanted a vegetable omelet. Mantuo Luo offered to go the Chinese supermarket for peppers, tomatoes, mushrooms, scallions, etc.

I scurried to the living room and retrieved her notebook. Pages and pages of words in Mandarin. Images of international spies with their miniature cameras photographing secret documents flashed in my mind. I adjusted my iPhone and took snapshots.

Mantuo Luo returned with the provisions. She fried diced vegetables in sesame oil, spiced them with dill, sage, rosemary, black pepper, and soy sauce poured the liquefied eggs.

We had breakfast watching an astronomy documentary on her Sony Bravia W8508 Premium Series flat TV screen. Spectroscopes indicated no traces of life on Phobos. That moon of Mars looked like a Grand Canyon with winds blowing in excess of eight hundred miles an hour. Methane and ammonia constituted its atmosphere. It looked like the surface had been swept clean. It was barren and hostile. A senator from Kentucky was lobbying to stop a federal grant to explore that planet.

Translations

The office of Jeffrey Donar, professor of Chinese linguistics at Columbia University, was a sanctuary for archival books. Stacks of old student's papers littered the floor. On an ornate Chinese table, a brass samovar flaunting a dragon with a demonic mouth as spout glistened in the afternoon light.

He was an elderly man, professorial with his rimless glasses and a silver goatee. His smiling face welcomed me as I entered his office. He pressed the dragon's forked tongue and poured steaming jasmine tea into two bowls.

"The Chinese drink tea scalding hot," he remarked as he ingested the burning infusion.

"I have translated the document you brought me. It's a log, the chronicles of a woman, living under the shadow of history. It's a collection of notes, reflections, observations. Well written. The author has literary talents, pure poetry, no problem getting published," he praised as he handed me the stapled script of the translation.

"Who is this woman?" he asked.

"Just a friend."

"May I meet her? She needs a literary agent, you know."

"I don't think she wants to be published."

"Does she know you gave me her writing for translation?"

"No," I confessed.

"You're a doppelganger!"

"I know."

"Are you going to tell her?" he asked.

"I don't think so."

"Think about your conscience and her trust in you," he pressed.

"What conscience? Thank you for your services."

I retreated.

I crossed the George Washington Bridge and entered the Palisades Parkway. I parked the car at an embankment.

Ruins of the Heart
Even Weeds Long for the Sun

"*Life is a question of relationships, not moral judgments, and you have to realize that a new relationship alters all the others that came before it*" *(Alberto Moravia).*

There is a motherland, a place of birth for the soul. Those who are fortunate to locate it spend felicitous lives free of inner discord. They are the inheritors, those who live in grace. Some find that hearth in their vocation, others in the trail of a dream, others in the amber liquid inside a bottle, others in the submission to a higher authority like so many of my brethren, others in the erotic fusion with another, others in God, etc. Those who do not enter that motherland are doomed to roam the earth, uprooted and restless, like disembodied spirits. I am one of these shadows walking the earth.

They, the Westerners, say childhood colors the rest of our days. Moments in infancy transformed and exalted in the kiln of the self visit us in altered forms, reconfiguring the present. What makes for a happy childhood? Understanding parents? A forgiving mother? A tolerant father? I have not been blessed on these accounts.

My childhood was not an anchorage, a port of call. It was dominated by my father, a man I venerated. "Sacrifice," he used to say, was Mao Zedong's gift to the Chinese people. His faith in Chairman Mao was unbreakable. I strove to embrace his unattainable standards. I grew accustomed to that climate of inevitable attainments. To this day, I hold all that is rotten with my life with his name.

I stopped reading, feeling guilty I was intruding on her private self. I was impressed by the sophistication of her text. I continued reading pages after pages.

I walked out of the car, eager for night air. The city in the distance glimmered. The sky shimmered. I wanted to locate her star. I remembered it was about right of the North Star. I spotted Polaris and searched in that vicinity. There was a multitude of points of light congregating in that quadrant of the sky.

I turned on the classical station in my car radio. The melody from Bizet's "Les Pecheurs de Perles" entranced the moment. My phone purred. She wanted to meet at a bar.

The Anvil on Eleventh Avenue and Thirteenth Street was a vast dingy basement under a decrepit building zoned for demolition, an apt location for a secret execution. The journey downstairs to this underground cellar was illuminated with strawberry-red and lime-green strobe lights. I was assaulted by throbbing electronic house music. It was a place patronized by people who wanted to get hammered. Drag queens in miniskirts danced on the bar. Guys in aluminum foil boxer shorts shimmered, their bodies greased, kaleidoscopes reflecting neon lights. Shemales in garters and push-up bras were talking to a group of businessmen in Brooks Brothers suits. A woman with rhinestones-studded panties cornered me, offering services. Sensing resistance, she proposed another item in her lascivious menu. Confronted with my silence, she propositioned a trip to Hershey Highway. A flamboyant boy nudged me: "Why so grumpy?" he asked with a Marilyn Monroe voice, brushing the strand of his wig against my face. A waiter, undressed like an adolescent Hermes with a winged helmet, roller-skated toward me.

"I'm here to meet someone," I said.

"Aren't we all?"

He fleeted away, mixing with the dancing crowd.

Couples fused, immersed in interminable kisses. Ravenous tongues wiggled inside humid mouths. Shadows shifted in dimly lit rooms. A scent of iron rust, lubricating jellies, and stale sweat permeated the stagnant air. The sound of rhythmic breathing, skin slapping skin echoed in that airless space. In the mucus darkness, hands stroked hardened flesh, fingers tickled moist protuberances, penetrated valleys, rubbed ridges.

I carved a path through humid torsos and cannabis clouds. I spotted her at the edge of the bar, nursing a drink. She was wearing a jogging suit with dark sneakers; she looked like a black panther on a tree branch.

"What're we doing here?" I asked.

She looked at me mistily.

"Horror is everywhere! It's the rule, not the exception. In China, all these misfits would have been arrested and given long sentences for indecency. Here, they can live out their fantasies," she voiced.

"There you are," my waiter on roller skates said. "You found your Circe. Compliment of the house," he said, handing me a drink.

She produced a pack of clove cigarettes.

"I didn't know you smoked."

"It's herbal," she claimed.

The barman in fishnet stockings and T-shirt clicked his lighter and ignited her cigarette.

"You like it here?" I asked, getting impatient.

"Yes," she said, offering me her lit cigarette.

Clove particles bit my tongue. Tiny slivers of cardamom mutilated my gums. I took several puffs.

"I'm thirsty," I moaned.

"We don't serve water here. I can get you Jamaican ginger," the barman said.

"Jamaican ginger!"

"Do you believe in animal reincarnation?" a patron mouthed.

"No!"

"I was a monkey on a banyan tree in the rain forest of Borneo," he dropped.

The clove cigarette and Jamaican ginger ale are deliriants. I spun around on the revolving stool and watched the dancers gyrate on the glittering dance floor. They were fluid in their movements, bereft of an endoskeleton. Everyone had soft bones in this enclosure. Their choreography was nonhuman, carnal, indicative of primate phylogeny. Leather grinding against chains, denim rubbing against zippers. They flung against each other, cosmic refuse, mangy romance, the skanky love life of reshuffled elements of the periodic table, elective affinities, blind cravings to fuse and generate new amalgams, orgy of muons and quarks. The bar was a hadron collider. Patrons in this gay, transsexual, S&M bondage club were gyrating to a hallucinated DJ looking for that Higgs boson element they call the god particle.

    I left her there and went back to my car. I was disillusioned in my Mantuo. She was visiting the underbelly of New York. And it looked like she liked it like a kid at FAO Schwarz. I understood that, having been sensorially deprived in her homeland for so long, she was letting loose, nourishing her anorectic imagination with intense experiences.

The Sludge

"*The sludge caught in the mind's filter, the stuff that refuses to go through, frequently becomes each person's obsession,*" Stephen King, a novelist more acquainted with human psyche than the founding fathers of modern psychology, once said.

I opted for the security of a public place, a battlefield, the site for the duel between Menelaos and Paris.

Cafe Dante is an Italian joint in the heart of Greenwich Village. The painted murals told a tale of unrequited love, a painted agony. A scene from the *Divine Comedy* illustrates the western wall of the main room. Dante Alighieri is strolling the Ponte Vecchio in Florence. Beatrice crossing the bridge from the opposite shore catches his attention. Inner wonders buried in his heart are stirred by her beauty, a felicity of flesh and spirit. He feels the pawing in his chest. He presses his hand on his convulsing heart, the fulcrum of his turmoil.

I have chosen this crime scene to meet Alvard, a rival I used to love, a man who pined for the same woman.

There were few customers eating gelato when I walked in. I chose a corner table away from the traveled alleys when I realized Alvard was already there, crouching near a window. He had arrived first in the battlefield, following Napoleon's strategy that you bring the battle to your enemy.

He was propped up in his chair like a ventriloquist's doll, body-punched. His chin was grainy, unshaven, his eyes shiny. They might as well have been glass.

"I haven't seen you around at the hospital. Where have you been?" I asked.

"Traveling abroad?" he said, his face beset by tremors.

"Where did you go?"

"Peru."

"Vacation?"

"I've been looking at alternative medical solutions."

He stared at me with an accusatory gaze.

"I know between you and Mantuo Luo."

His eyes were drills.

"I introduced her to you. You abducted her and sequestered her in some hole in Queens."

I didn't reply, preferring the ramparts of silence.

"It's over," he growled.

"What're talking about?"

"She cured your asthma. Let her go."

"She can leave anytime," I said.

"I need her," he said.

Alvard unbuttoned his shirt and exposed his chest. Islands of redness pockmarked his skin.

"I have a rash, I have a fucking rash. It's back. I consulted dermatologists. Blood work negative. They promised further studies. Further studies, my ass. I know what it is. I couldn't tell them my theory, that my skin is upset, it's having a tantrum. My skin is crying, man."

He paused. I was alarmed by his eyes, opaque and gray, the eyes of a deep-sea organism.

A thought came to me that shed light on his perturbation. Alvard had made his own bachelor life a series of narrow escapes from amorous alliances. He was focusing on Mantuo Luo as his panacea.

"I have to resume the treatment, damn it! This skin condition doesn't respond to any medication. I explored alternative medicine, herbs, vitamins, minerals. I stumbled into this book, *Touching* by Ashley Montagu. It's the relationship between skin contact and stimulation and physical and emotional diseases. Amazing read! It says that infants and children who are not touched, hugged, caressed, stroked, rubbed in the early years develop all kinds of psychosomatic disorders and internal organs malfunctions. Astounding chapter on pulmonary, hepatic, and renal inadequacies connected to epidermic and cutaneous sensorial deprivation. They should make this book a requirement in medical school. I was an adopted child, you know, into a family who took me in for the monthly government subsidies they received. Mantuo Luo took care of a need that had never been fulfilled. She fed this epidermic hunger. That's how I can explain the therapeutic impact of her touch."

He got quiet, introspective. I realized his starvation. No mother ever made him feel like the axis of her universe.

"My skin has become accustomed to her touch."

"Why don't you continue your skin treatment with another competent masseuse?" I proposed.

"It's not the same, it's imprinting. My skin got used to her hands. My skin remembers her," he clamored.

"What about Farhana?"

"It's over."

"Maybe you didn't give it a chance."

"She's not the mother type. I have no use for an Arab intellectual who knows it all. I want to see Mantuo."

"She doesn't do massage anymore," I said.

"You'll ruin her talent. She's a gift from God, and I don't believe in God."

"She doesn't want to spend her days rubbing men's backs. Can you blame her?" I protested.

I drifted, distracted by images of their lovemaking. I saw Alvard pouncing on her, scavenging her flesh. I imagined his murky tongue, curling inside her dark corners, his cock probing her underworld. I wanted to plant my fork in his carotid artery.

"I led you to the Grail, and you want to keep it for yourself," he hammered.

The air in the room coagulated, making breathing a chore.

"Lend her to me," he demanded.

"Lend her? What is she, a lawn mower?"

I tried hard not to let my rage mangle my words.

"You know, Gabriel, I could do a lot of damage," he threatened.

"What do you mean?"

Up north, clouds gave out a loud roll of thunder, like a circus drummer before some acrobatic feat.

I bit my lips to quell the blossoming rage. My ears filled with a thousand dins. We were both living on a fault line that could open at any moment.

"I have videos of both of you lovebirds in this fancy Italian restaurant, sucking tongues at the planetarium. I don't want to hurt Mantuo Luo. To expose your affair with your masseuse will wreck her life and yours."

"You had us followed? I don't believe it."

"What do you expect?"

"You want to destroy what you cannot have."

"You have interfered with my treatment by taking away my healer. Look at the big picture," he grumbled.

Alvard paused. He picked up a candy from his pants pocket, unwrapped it.

"You're my friend, my best friend."

He paused, looking at me inquisitively.

"She complained about you, you know," he said.

"I doubt it."

"Think of your wife, Maren. She'll find out one day. It'll reap her heart out. Think of your marriage, your career."

"Don't go there!"

"Imagine yourself as a fish, working a hook deeper and deeper into your bleeding jaw. You hypnotized this refugee just off the boat. She comes to New York to seek refuge just to fall into your trap. I bet you, you thought you could by her with your money. You got her an apartment, I bet you give her an allowance. Weekly, monthly? You convinced her to leave her job, what she's good at. You promised you'd support her. What that makes you? A sugar daddy with a sugar baby. She's your slave, right? Human trafficking."

"You're way over your head."

"I could send an anonymous letter to the FBI. There'll be a knock on the door. There would be an investigation. You don't want the Department of Immigration and Naturalization to poke its nose in her entry visa. Or the IRS. You don't want her to be tax audited. They'd haul her to jail. They'll deport her. Think what I could do to your China doll."

Alvard, a brutal little smirk distorting his facial muscles, ambled away. My mood was in the cellar.

I was rereading Cioran the other night, and I found this great saying: *"The interesting thing about friendship is that it is, almost as much as love, an inexhaustible source of disappointment and outrage."*

Ritual

Every Sunday night, ritualistically, my wife sits on a yellow sofa in the living room to watch television. She's selective and particular in her viewing menu. These last few weeks, her attention had been riveted by a *Showtime* series: *The Affair*. My presence is required for this screening. This encounter brings us close. It generates lively discussions. Maren derives a great deal of pleasure in critiquing each episode, deconstructing the plot, analyzing the characters, etc.

Watching this visual illustration of a marital deception on a giant screen in the middle of our living room fills me up with dread. Every Sunday, with apprehension bordering on panic, at 10:00 p.m., I watch these doomed characters. As I am involved in a liaison in the periphery of my marriage, I compare myself with the fictional individuals of the story as they struggle against a multitude of obstacles, internal vicissitudes, external hindrances. At times, I embrace these lost souls with empathy, identify with their criminality and vulnerability. At other times, I become a harsh judge condemning their delinquency.

The Affair is the story of Noah, a schoolteacher and struggling novelist, who is married to Helen, the daughter of a successful novelist who subsidizes his son-in-law's family expenses. Noah takes his brood for a summer vacation in scenic Montauk in Long Island. The monotony of his insipid life is incinerated by the appearance of Alison, a waitress at the local seafood restaurant. Alison is married to Cole, a resident of this seaside town. Every character conceals secrets.

After we watched the suspenseful last segment, in an introspective mood enhanced by chilled sauvignon blanc, my wife opened the predictable inquiry.

"What do you think of Noah?"

"He's a sad sack," I said.

"Why do you say that?"

"He's a narcissist, selfish, and nearsighted. And he shouldn't have left his wife. She's a great girl."

"What do you mean?"

"You don't leave your wife for your mistress unless you are married to Medusa," I said.

I meant everything I was saying. My wife was comforted by my philosophy, the value I was giving to loyalty.

"Why does he leave a fine wife, a great mother with four kids, for an uneducated waitress?" she asked.

"Because she's a wounded bird, and he needs a project, a mission." I launched.

She paused and sipped her wine.

"Do you feel you need a project?"

"I have more projects that I can handle. Every day I create an objective, a target. I want to save a life, and sometimes I succeed."

"How do you feel when you lose a patient?"

"A part of me dies with them. You see, I got a perfect job for a manic-depressive."

"You were diagnosed by a psychiatrist?"

"No, I self-diagnosed myself."

"Maybe you should take some meds?"

"It's not that bad, you know. My job doesn't help. Some patients give up the ghost while I'm doing my job! I'm down for days."

"You never talk about that."

"I don't want to depress you."

"I want to help you when things are getting tough for you."

"I'm touched. A piece of cake will do wonders for my manic depression right now."

"I have a French apple tart in the fridge. I'll go get some. Do you want some coffee with it?"

"Sure."

She returned with a slice.

"There's an expression, if you say 'Somebody doesn't have both oars in the water,' what does it mean exactly?" she asked.

"Means the guy is wacko, nuts, off, not completely there."

"Alvard stopped by yesterday," Maren said.

It felt like a slap. I was unprepared.

"He was here?"

"Yes."

"He didn't call?"

"No."

"Why didn't you tell me?"

"I don't know. I didn't want to upset you."

"What did he want?"

"A patient was assigned to him. He wants her back."

"Why is he talking to you about it?"

"He said he tried to talk to you. You don't have both oars in the water. He'd go to higher authorities," he said.

"Who are they these higher authorities? It's the patient's right to choose her doctor. Case closed," I clamored.

I was furious at Alvard's impertinence, to bring a private matter to my home, to my wife and use her influence. The audacity, the arrogance of his blackmail. He was letting me know he could at any point expose my affair and do serious damage.

"Who is this patient?" Maren asked.

I figured the best way to hide the complete truth of a situation is to offer a morsel of the story without exposing the core.

"That patient is an Asian girl with a history of uterine cysts. I think Alvard has another agenda, to deflower Madame Butterfly," I said.

"Is she beautiful?" she asked.

"Classic Asian face, very bland," I replied.

"I'm tired. I'm going to bed," she said, eager to abandon the inquiry.

My wife didn't want to get embroiled in the conspiracies that men hatch. Her lack of paranoid ideation was remarkable. A little more entanglement would have pleased me; a bit more drama I would have found entertaining. It would satisfy my bipolarity. Is my marital stability a factor in my delinquency, and did Maren's lack of jealousy and possessiveness have something to do with my transgression?

A Glance from Her

At Barnes & Noble, I bought many books of Chinese poetry in translation. I preferred the Han Dynasty poet Li Yannian:

>*In the North there is a beauty*
>*Surpassing the world*
>*She stands alone*
>*A glance from her*
>*Will overthrow a city*
>*Another glance*
>*Will overthrow a nation*
>*It is difficult to behold*
>*Such a beauty again*

Antiheroes

Few days later, my wife wanted to talk about Noah, the protagonist from the TV show *The Affair*. She liked the guy. Some women go for wounded sparrows.

The last few years, American television began featuring antiheroes. These protagonists committed great acts of destruction yet experienced empathic and compassionate emotions toward others, people they protected. American audiences felt affection for Dexter, a serial killer who dispatched many undesirables; Tony Soprano, a mafioso family man who tried being a good father; Brody, a tortured American soldier in a show entitled *Homeland* and Walter White from *Breaking Bad*. The viewing public received an instruction in the pliability of evil and the malleability of ethics. The results of these movies on the American psyche cannot be underestimated. The viewers understood the nature of evil and sided with these seductive misfits. This new tolerance for the unpredictability and irrationality of the human soul expanded their consciousness, and they became living room philosophers. Because of my questionable actions, did I become an ambulatory psychopath like so many television heroes who grace our screens?

I Am Hallucinating

A singularity manifested itself during surgery yesterday. I had opened the uterus of a woman with a severe case of endometriosis. Her endometrium had spread to her ovaries and invaded the uteral space. A miniature boy was crouching inside that matrix like that Greek philosopher Diogenes, who lived inside a large clay barrel in Alexandria. The boy's name was Narcissus. He wanted to know if he should extend his embryonic life in the womb or be delivered and face the great outdoors. I recommended he should exit this cramped space and be born. "It's going to hurt," I murmured. I must have mouthed those words out loud, because the head anesthesiologist confirmed the anesthesia was going well and the patient I was operating wasn't feeling anything. I apologized for my comment and hurriedly completed my work.

Visiting Mother

I drove to the flower district, Sixth Avenue and Twenty-Eighth Street. Trucks were unloading massive bouquets of long-stemmed flowers. Blossoming trees from flatbeds were hauled to the pavements where they are tagged and numbered for delivery to the rooftops of penthouses. Stores displayed flowers of exotic origins, luxuriant bushes and overflowing shrubs exported from the Orient, trees with shiny leaves, colorful vines. I sauntered into the leafy grove, inebriated by the visual overload of colors. I navigated alleys of blossoms.

I entered a verdant showroom. If I get Mother a bouquet after a few days, petals would wilt, stems would lose their vigor, and Mother would throw them away. A potted plant would last, re-creating itself with new buds. A green bush with elongated white flowers, trumpetlike, hanging like chimes attracted my attention. I had seen that plant before. In my masseuse's salon, the Buddha in the Chinese screen was holding a bundle of these white flowers. I asked the florist. He praised its hardiness. This plant is very adaptable. It thrived indoors as well outdoors and blossomed at night. "Strange thing," he commented. I chose it. One of his men put it in my trunk.

Nyack is a postcard village north of New York in Rockland County. For her seventieth birthday, I had offered my mother a house by the water. It was a modest dwelling with a wooden deck with a majestic view of the Hudson. She cultivated a culinary herb garden that scented the neighborhood. I had a greenhouse built for her where she grew spices that usually blossomed in Malabar and Sri Lanka. Under her care, they proliferated in the glasshouse. Her sharing, with her neighbors, of cloves, cinnamon, cardamom, and vanilla seeds earned her a well-deserved reputation among her vegetarian friends in the neighborhood. She didn't pursue the cultivation of flowers. Beauty, she mistrusted. Flowers intimidated her. She used to quote a Zulu proverb: "Don't choose the flowery plants but fruit bearing ones." I carried the pot into the living room and removed the paper wrap exposing the plant.

"What beautiful flowers," she said, embracing the pot.

I was surprised. The adoption was a success.

"I made ginger and cinnamon tea," she said.

We sat down in the sunroom surrounded by ivy climbing on bamboo reeds sprouting from flamboyant Chinese pots.

"How are you, Mother?"

"I'm fine. And you? I've got Rehrucken in the oven. It's not ready yet."

"What is it?"

"A glazed chocolate sponge cake filled with apricot jam and studded with almonds. That's for dessert."

"Sounds delicious! How's your health?" I asked.

"I'm just fine. And how's your asthma?"

"It's much better. I'm getting massage. Amazing results."

"I'm happy you're feeling better."

A cannonade of clouds in the distance was approaching Nyack.

"Are you lonely, Mother?" I asked.

"I have company," she said, pointing a finger at her house plants.

"Quiet friends."

"They have their own language, you know. I know it sounds mystical or an old woman with dementia, but every living thing speaks to other living things."

"Are you a plant whisperer now, Mother?"

"I wouldn't say that. I just feel less lonely when I'm near them, you know?"

"It's like having a pet. I get it."

"Yeah, that's right."

"Are you going to show me the greenhouse?"

We walked out of the house to the backyard and into the glasshouse. Inside was a miniature rain forest, steamy, humid. Luxuriant leaves grew from potted plants. Stems and branches formed a canopy in this pocket-size jungle.

"The Bronx Botanical Garden should offer you a job."

"I wouldn't give up my children, no way," she said.

"Well, I can see they're doing well. Good parenting!"

"Why don't you grow flowers?" I asked.

"Well, son, would you invite an old lady to a party thrown by adolescent girls?"

"You're still very beautiful, Mother."

"I don't want to compete," she said with a little laughter.

"I got you this flowering bush. You are okay with it."

"I'm glad you did. Having one flowering plant, I can live with that." Her mood lifted.

We drank the herbal tea.

"I'm sorry. I should visit you more often," I said.

"Your life is hard. The patients you have to take care of, hospital duties, a wife at home, a daughter—I understand."

"No excuses."

Somewhere in the atmosphere, high above the Catskills cumuli packed with electricity collided in spectacles of light and sound. In the amber light of dusk, the surrounding walls jaundiced.

"It's going to rain soon. It's strange, the weather channel didn't predict any rain. What do they know?"

She poured more tea in my cup.

"One of these days, I'm going to open Dad's chest you gave me," I announced.

"I never looked inside, you know," she said.

"Dad wrote a diary. Do you want to have a look at it?" I asked.

"I don't know."

"You sure?"

"There are secrets, I'm sure."

"You told me Dad spent some time in India."

"He didn't want anyone to know he had cancer. The oncologist said it would take about two years. Your father bought a one-way ticket to Varanasi."

"The City of the Dead?"

"He became a mortuary assistant. He prepared the funeral pyres and cremated the dead. He said he never felt so free in his life. And then one day, the letters stopped coming. The Indian authorities sent me their condolences. They sent me an urn containing his ashes. I buried his ashes in the military cemetery. Do you want to know what's for dinner?"

"Of course, Mother."

"I've made a dish you never had before: Thai chicken curry with vegetables."

"Sounds grand!"

Mother left and returned with plates. She set the table and brought her best crystal glasses.

We sat in the shadow of a dwarf eucalyptus tree in the darkening room and savored this Asian dish.

The evening flowed magically.

"Have you read the news?" she asked.

"I don't have time to read."

"They found Samantha Waters."

She handed me the *New York Post*. It said: "*A body of a fifteen-year-old teenager was unearthed by a backhoe excavating the backyard of a residence belonging to a deceased known drug dealer. The body was in a state of extreme decomposition. Dental records identified the victim as Samantha Waters.*"

There were photographs of the parents smothering tears.

I remembered Samantha's face.

"I'm sorry, son," Mother muttered.

I don't know why, I didn't feel anything.

Dusk was coloring the sky a pale burned sienna when I left Mother and headed toward the Tappan Zee Bridge. In the middle of the bridge, the traffic stopped. Within minutes, police cruisers, sirens whining, were trying desperately to reach the flash point. I saw a police officer running from car to car, talking to the drivers. A voice magnified by a bullhorn reverberated. The police needed a medical person to talk to a man who parked his 18-wheeler truck in the middle of the bridge and, climbing the metal beams of the bridge to the top, was threatening to jump. I introduced myself. Officer Ocallahan was the officer on duty. He looked young and overwhelmed. It was his first encounter with a suicide case. I showed him my credentials. I'd try to talk to the crazy guy.

A fork of lightning flowed from the firmament illuminating the skeleton of the bridge,

Borrowing the officer's binoculars, I spotted the psycho perched on the top of an iron rafter.

I took off my suit jacket and handed it to the police officer. I grabbed the bullhorn and began the ascent of the bridge. The climb was arduous and dangerous. It wasn't a smart thing to do at my age. I'm not a rock climber, for heaven's sake. Why was I getting involved with this? I was hoping my wife and my daughter were not watching TV. I finally got to the guy astride a beam. I was breathing heavily like a rented mule.

"Hey!" I yelled.

"Who're you?" the broken voice rattled.

"Move your truck! You're blocking the goddamn traffic!"

"Fuck your mother, asshole. I'm going to jump."

"The rains are coming. Where's your umbrella?"

"Are you psycho, dude?"

"I am! So why didn't he jump already?"

"You're going to tell me when to jump?"

"You're not going to jump! You like the attention a lot!"

"Oh yeah, I'm going to show you!" he launched.

"I got a better idea, dude!"

"Yeah?"

"Hear me out! It's your lucky day! I'm going to make you a hero, man. You'll be in all the papers tomorrow."

"Stop jerking me off!"

"You're going to be famous today!"

"What are you FBI, Homeland Security? Navy SEAL?"

"Naw! Look over there, the news vans, NBC, FOX, ABC. Look, they even got BBC. And the helicopter, that's Channel 11. They're all here for you. Let's give them something to talk about."

"Talk about what?"

"You got their attention, man. When does that happen to anybody in one's lifetime? Never ever! You'll get millions of people watching the news on their TV set, looking at your face and listening to you talk. Do want to grab that opportunity of a lifetime?"

"I don't know?"

"Hey, man, you got to make up your mind, we don't got the whole night. The more you stay here, the more people are going to get pissed off. They want to drive home and eat their lasagna, but they can't on account you blocked the bridge with your truck."

"Are you shooting a commercial? I'm going to be in the ad?"

"I'm no adman. Now you got all people excited. They're betting right now: you're going to jump, or you're not going to jump. All the cameras are waiting. They hope you hit the water hard, so they get that money shot. That's the footage they want to get. Make their day, go ahead, jump! Get your body to hit that water at ninety miles an hour, bang or live and make buckets of money."

"What do you say?"

"You're trying to get their attention. Things are bad in the Big Apple. New Yorkers are angry, disgruntled, because the city ain't working right. You just need the light the fuse of all that anger they store inside, and it's a short fuse. Remember, you're mad as hell and you're not going to take it anymore, right?"

"Okay," he bellowed.

"You take the bullhorn, and I'll be your prompter."

"What's that?"

"He's the guy in the theater who tells the words to the actor who forgot his lines. I'll tell you what to say, and you just repeat my words into this gadget so the people down there hear it. The news guys will record it, and it'll flash in the six o'clock news. Ready?"

"I don't know! It's weird!"

"Here we go. Repeat after me, and sound real mad. Okay? Here we go!"

"I'm just like you, guys! I love this city, but I'm fed up with hobos, the stinking homeless, vagrants sleeping in subway platforms, alcoholics on crack who run over babies in strollers, psychos walking the streets, the government-subsidized walking dead, guys slashing commuters at bus stops, mental patients released from underfunded city psychiatric wards jabbing pedestrians, pushing travelers on the paths of the D train. We are the people in New York. New Yorkers are disgusted with the police commissioner's victory speeches and statistics that crime is in decline in the five boroughs, my ass, killings are in an all-time high. Tired of the economic injustice, they're building these tall glass buildings and selling apartments to rich Russians and Asians who buy them as investments. Nobody lives there. They stay empty, while the homeless sleep in the street and die of pneumonia in the dead of winters, the city-subsidized, rodent-infested apartments in Queens and Brooklyn in neighborhood invaded by gangs of armed meth merchants. I'm sick to hear about our sons being fondled by the Catholic priests, and they keep on preaching after their superiors are told. Do you know the Catholic Church owes more real estate in New York than any of these land barons? Why don't they open some of their buildings to the poor, the wretched of the earth? But nobody cares. My wife dumped me because I wasn't home enough. The fact I was driving trucks from Kansas City to New York, doing a double shift to make enough money for my autistic daughter—that didn't matter to her, so she starts some shenanigan with our babysitter. She said she's a liberated girl—my wife a lesbian and a fucking pedophile, a nice Irish girl from Maspeth, Queens. The mayor couldn't care less, the city movers and shakers hide in their Hamptons, while stray bullets cut down infants in their strollers. I've had it. I'm mad as hell, and I won't take it anymore."

Suddenly, all the motorists got out of their cars and applauded like it was New Year's Eve in Times Square.

"I told you so. Look over there—news trucks. Look, ABC, NBC, CNN—they're filming you. They got everything on tape. You're the man of the hour. Now they all cheer for you. Come down and let's go shake some hands and sign some autographs. You got your hour of fame, dump your wife. Now you get your pick of the liter."

"For real?"

"Look at them! They're eating it up! Now you got to move your truck to the garage. The cops will arrest you 'cause you blocked the bridge and you created a scandal. They'll keep you in jail for a day or two, then they'll release you. They got to. The media will go after them. But you'll get a lot of free publicity. You'll be invited to all the talk shows. Philanthropy organizations will hire you. You'll be the toast of the town."

"I don't know what to say, man."

"Don't mention it."

He jumped from the railing and began his descent. Journalists and fans were delirious. I walked to my car and waited for the crowd to disperse. He moved his truck and drove away escorted by five police vans, sirens blazing, followed by a dozen TV vans.

I drove home. When I got home, Miou received me with welcoming purrs. I opened a can of mackerel puree. I filled a tumbler with Jack Daniel's. I turned the TV on and collapsed in the La-Z-Boy. The anchorwoman, an incarnation of Latina femininity, announced "*a miracle on the Tappan Zee Bridge.*" She was reporting about this trucker who had blocked the bridge for hours. He climbed the bridge to commit suicide apparently, but a Good Samaritan climbed after him. The suspect then delivered a speech of all that was wrong with the city to a cheering audience. He was taken for questioning. A big crowd formed outside the police station and demanded his immediate release. The press has praised the bravery of that citizen who climbed the bridge to talk to the suicidal man. The police is trying to find the identity of that man who spoke to a policeman on duty. The officer claimed he's a doctor. The TV people worked the streets of New York to get the reaction of the people to the speech of that man. The pedestrians they talked to couldn't agree with the guy more: the only way to get some attention from the indifferent city government and public officials is to stage a demonstration, a show. The mayor was interviewed and promised reforms. Bill Gates and Jeff Bezos donated millions to Meals on Wheels.

I fell asleep on the La-Z-Boy.

I dreamed of colonnades and arches. Spectators genuflecting in prayers and meditations. My bleached skin contrasted with the brown bodies of visitors and tonsured priests. I bathed my body in the waters of the Ganges. Devotees were mixing red cinnabar powder in small mortars, preparing to paint their forehead. On the pavement, corpses wrapped in red, shrouded others in white, awaited their turn to be cremated. The red wrapping were women; white cloth for the men. Relatives and priests were throwing butter and incense on corpses. I saw my corpse wrapped in white, borne on a bamboo litter, and escorted by chanting rishis. It was placed on a pile of wood. A devotee lit the fire with a torch he had ignited at the sacred fire at the Shiva Temple. Black powdery particles danced in the smoke. Flesh sizzled as it burned making music. The purification, the returning my body to its mineral ingredients continued. Although I was burning, I felt no sadness.

I woke up, my body sweating as if from a tropical fever.

Visiting the Dead

I read about funeral flowers. The lily represented rebirth of the departed soul; the orchid portrayed honor. I discounted carnations which designate innocence. I chose gentians, blue flowers. They lit the path of any visitor to the underworld. So said Homer. Armed with a bouquet of gentians, I drove to the Calverton Military Cemetery. After Mother told me of my dad's last two years as a funeral pyre apprentice in the city by the Ganges, I wanted to visit this man who raised me.

White tombstones arranged like dominoes met me.

A family was standing in front of a gravestone.

They had brought the family terrier for that special outing. The dog was whining, crying, scratching the patch of grass. It inhaled its master's decaying flesh few feet under, pawing the dirt, digging a tunnel to his master's body. Two men in uniforms were standing in a frozen military salute. They were staring at the slabstone, drawn inexorably to the name carved in the marble plate. Yards away, a mother, her infant in a carriage, crouched on the gravel. With a soapy sponge, she was washing the slab. The infant giggled, stretching her hands. The mother took the child out of the carriage and put the sponge in her tiny hand.

I continued my errand down the alleys. At the bottom of a hill, a young man was urinating on a tombstone, a son's revenge. A throng of visitors formed a semicircle around a minister. The group comprised several families. The women in elegant black dresses and the men in their dignified dark suits stood with their heads down. The clergyman intoned a prayer for the dead.

"From the book of Maccabees in the Old Testament, 'It is a holy and wholesome thought to pray for the dead, that they may be loosed from sins,' 2 Maccabees 12:46."

Prayer releases us from sins. Is that a fact? I have my doubts about the rescue from easy metaphysics.

Guided by the map, I followed down designated alleys until I got to Elm Street, lot number 10,459. My father resided in this permanent site impervious to time and space, transcending history he had helped shape. I felt close to him. The dead had come to the rescue the living. I placed the bouquet by the gravestone and sat on the grass.

I thought of Mantuo. In this mortuary field, when one would expect to be immune to the intrusion of earthly concerns. I felt her gaze, remote, aloof, detached. She was there, spectral, like a hologram, a silhouette diaphanous like a halo shimmering over slabstones. Her face, how each of her features laid in perfect harmony with every other: the arch of her pencil-line eyebrows echoing those of her lips, her linear nose receiving correction from the swooning curve of her neck. It was the way she looked at me, the radiance emanating out of the infinite depth of her eyes. I imagined my father kissing her, tasting eternity. The commingling of tongues, the insistence of fingers exploring with the ardor of a Crusader digging for relics in the desert sand of the Holy Land. What immortality her extraordinary forehead foretold? I wish my father had met Mantuo Luo. To have witnessed her imperious stare before he died. He would have felt like a saint welcoming the stigmata. I wasn't the sole spectator and martyr. My father, who walked with death in the killing fields of Europe, had become a fellow traveler in my pilgrim's progress.

The Ardennes

My wife wasn't home. She was visiting a friend who had triumphed in a competitive triathlon. A celebration party was organized in the athlete's honor. Maren invited me to the shindig. I declined. I ventured into the garage, which had become a memorabilia depot. I spotted the large chest. I opened the sesame and contemplated the relics. Inside the metallic safe, Hitler Youth's scarves wrapped German military paraphernalia, Nazi insignias, Gestapo medals, a Luger and a Walther my father used for target practice. There were boxes of cartridges sealed and dated 1955.

There was a notebook. The green cover had marks, scratches, and tears. It had traveled and known the abuse of war. I opened its battered cardboard and faced the first page. *Commentaries* was scribbled in pencil. I was going to visit history, reported by an eyewitness, anecdotes of a sniper behind enemy lines. His journal was the confession of a trained murderer. It's a killing log.

Emboldened by a tumbler of Jack Daniel's, I ensconced myself in my favorite chair holding my father's diary. With trepidation, I opened the notebook at random.

> *My partner's blood had congealed during the night. I hardly knew him. He was a car salesman from Detroit. Snipers were in great demand. We came as a pair. We were ordered to clean out the forest of pockets of resistance before the advance of the foot soldiers. We spent most of the time hiding, invisible. Snipers are reptilian. They are alerted by motion. I'd rather freeze to death than be perforated by a 7.92 bullet from a Karabiner 98K. The rum-*

ble of a tank far away kindled hope. From the signature sound of the engine, I recognized the stutter of a Sherman, not a Panzer. It must have been a mile away.

The sky, black and misty, blanketed the foxholes. My lips were frosted. Icicles dangled from my nose. Hypothermia would succeed where the German sniper failed. The kraut was in the same dire straits: the cruel chill. He had spilled the blood of a midwestern boy and was brimming with Teutonic pride. Silence was oppressive. My breathing was at a minimum, just enough oxygen to keep my mind from shutting off. Eyes were useless. Hearing was sharpened. In the stillness of the woods, without the night animals on the hunt, sound travels. A vibration originated somewhere behind the bushes. Was it a branch falling from a tree, an empty rifle magazine falling on the ice? It came from a corner in the woods. I sealed my eyes with the SS scarf I had scavenged from a German officer I had dispatched couple of days ago to Valhalla. I tore the scarf and wrapped it around the muzzle. The anticipation of slaughter gave me an erection. I was the execution squad, Gabriel, the exterminating angel. Fury kept the fire in me well stoked. I peed inside my camouflage cargo pants. The piss warmed my thighs, invigorating my skin. My soul was cruising for a carnage. I didn't have to wait for the cloud to unblock the moon. I didn't have to wait for the fog to dissipate. I welcomed the dark. It was the last Lucky Strike in my pack. The last cigarette you smoke before the firing squad spatters your cerebellum. I ignited the cigarette with my army lighter and ducked just in time. I expected him to fire, and he did. His German bullet ripped through the air around me. It jolted me. I shot at the point of light in the dense foliage.

The Wild Wild West in a field in Belgium. A blast. I passed out. A hand was poking my chest.

"Wake up," the voice resonated.

Lieutenant Ambrosio from Bayridge, Brooklyn, grunted, grinning.

"You shot the bastard."

I stared at the officer, speechless.

"That was Linghauer, the guy Himler sent to kill us. He downed seven of ours. His bullet grazed your skull. You'd have bled to death, but your blood froze."

That day, I found out my father was a sniper during the war.

Kindled Spirit

Mantuo Luo invited me to the Buddhist Temple in Flushing, Queens.

A brass statue of the Buddha was occupying a niche in the wall. Frescoes of half-naked women in flamboyant sarongs wrapped around their hips in various dancing pauses illustrated the ceiling. Their faces were identical: elongated with slanting eyes, half opened with long eyebrows curved above them. There was a cold intelligence about their faces sharpened by their straight noses with slightly flaring nostrils. Their breasts were ripe pomegranates ready to burst. Some dancers were half reclining, with their backs turned, showing the enticing curve of their hips. Others revealed an overflowing sensual abdomen barely concealed. Mantuo gripped my hand, a promise in her gleaming eyes.

"What language is that?" I asked, pointing at a calligraphy in the ceiling.

"Siamese."

Gilded letters I couldn't identify, garnished, the ceiling painted in persimmon red.

She translated: *Unfertilized thinking brings death.*

"What does it mean?" I asked Mantuo.

"If you wish to live, you must not cling to purity. You must not cut yourself from all channels of retreat, you must not reject every path," she uttered.

I thought Buddhism was all about detachment, distancing from desire, a relief from cravings, quietude, and a bright stillness. Not this brand of Buddhism.

This temple exuded pure joy. This Siddhartha Gautama of the Sakyas knew the power of sex to kindle the spirit and advance in the journey toward liberation.

"*You only live twice. Once for the world, the other for your dreams*"—the words from a popular song from a James Bond movie.

"*What would I be without my obsessions? Plankton in the Arctic Sea?*" a French philosopher asked.

Everything I do with my body honors me. It's what I do with my mind that degrades me. When we must make a crucial decision, it is extremely dangerous to consult anyone else, since no one, with the exception of a few, wishes us well.

Death Be Not Proud

I am intimate with death. The hospital is a house of healing and a funeral station. Patients expire every day in every city hospital. I have, in spite of my efforts and the ardor of my surgical team, lost patients. I've not acquired an emotional armor, a detachment. But mostly I am a messenger of life, a champion of light. I am not a bringer of death, the Fourth Horseman of the Apocalypse. Yet, I conceived a crime: the assassination of a colleague.

Two Women

The French poet Florian said, "*The happy life is the hidden life.*" My life illustrates this aphorism. At times, I experienced the schism. I justified to myself the duality of my existence and maintained my divided self. Didn't I consider the negative impacts? In my profession, I saved souls. As a husband, I shined. My wife appreciated my companionship, my affection, my care. I endured her low sex drive and didn't become indignant at her passionless reality. I'm not being fair right now. My wife was a source of domestic bliss. She was also an athlete. As a yoga aficionado and practitioner, she had gathered a following of bright and creative women who adored her. Her energy made her soar to levels I could only dream of. My craving for intimate intensity was satisfied by my Chinese concubine. With her, I navigated forbidden sea. She wasn't an equal to Maren but her inferior. I recognized that. I was not noble or elevated; that's because in my justification in dignifying my human traits, I had not forgotten that in my arteries flowed the blood of monkeys.

Conversations with Walther P38

I revisited my father's trove of German memorabilia. This time, I wanted to get acquainted with his Walther P38. It was an attractive gun plated in matte black. Its caliber was 9 mm Parabellum, with eight round detachable magazines with an effective range of ninety-eight yards. It featured a safety indicator pin which showed whether there was a cartridge in the chamber or not. It was the sidearm of the officers of the Wehrmacht. I had never fired a gun before.

The next items on my agenda: the kill place. What makes a favorable crime scene? Criminals are apprehended because they select the wrong kill zone. I didn't sleep that night. We learn more from one white night than in a year of sleep. I thought of Richard III great lines: *I have it. It is engendered. Hell and night must bring this monstrous birth, to the world's light.* Getting acquainted with my father's firearm was the next thing to do.

The Walther P38 is a war trophy. Holding this relic in my hand and tightening my fingers around the trigger exhilarated me. I fired and missed the trunk of a birch some fifty yards away. The recoil rattled my shoulder. I pulled the trigger again and again, unleashing the genie out of the gun's magazine. I felt power coursing through my veins. A man could become addicted to this adrenaline rush. Statistics illustrate the extent of this craving. In 2014 handguns were responsible for 38, 587 dead in the US.

I was learning to shoot a gun to terminate a rival. Anger didn't belong in this equation. I didn't despise my opponent. In fact, I cared a great deal about him. I'd liquidate him, dispassionately. I'd to achieve that impartiality and detachment, the hallmark of great assassins. Miyamoto Musashi, the undefeated samurai who won sixty-five duels, refused to engage an opponent because he was too angry at him, canceling the encounter. That samurai became my model.

The Adirondack Park is a seven-hundred-thousand-acre forest.

During that afternoon, the forest resonated with the clash of thunder from my pistol. I fired continuously, improving my accuracy. After discharging sixty rounds, I'd developed a relationship with the firearm. I had subjugated it to my will. An understanding, an agreement between codependent allies had emerged. The organic and the mechanical were cooperating. I'd saved it from oblivion and decay. I'd given it another chance to affect human lives. It had been designed for that purpose: to assist humans in their destiny. It'd serve other masters. Its joie de vivre came to a halt when the war had ended. It was buried inside a coffer of war trophies, maybe for eternity. I exhumed it, breathed life into it, and extended its usefulness. This Walther had a new mission, a raison d'être. It owed its resurrection to me.

Into the Woods

Back at the hospital, a patient was scheduled for a kidney transplant. She was on standby, waiting for a donor. Alvard was managing the case. I was assigned to perform the surgery. There were some secondary health issues with the patient that concerned me. I was questioning her survivability. I dropped at Alvard's office to confer. His laptop was opened. The Harriman State Park website highlighted a camping ground.

A natural setting is a conducive environment for an execution. An ecological habitat, a wilderness without electronic surveillance cameras, and only a couple of underpaid rangers who patrol that territory corresponded with my design.

Palisades Parkway was a two-lane highway that paralleled the Hudson River. I always favored it for any journey upstate. I drove north to Route 6 west in its scenic splendor deep inside the Shawagunk Range at the feet of the Catskill Mountains.

It was cloudy with ashy patches of fog lingering like low flying clouds. I felt sullen, morose. Meteorology determines the color of my mood. In the park, nature was in full regalia. Elms, hulking oaks, leafy maples, and majestic birches escorted me through a dense underbrush. An abundant foliage, grandiose rock formations, gorges, and small canyons dotted my path. My murderous intent faltered in this a serene landscape. Harmony in nature is a complete illusion. I had been deceived by TV eco-evangelists who assert that in nature, all is for the best, whereas the worst has corrupted flora and faunae, and in the natural world in a very real sense, all is for the worst. Unseen by mortal eyes within a radius of ten feet, a praying mantis is shredding a bee, a basilica orbweaver spider is injecting her stomach acids inside the abdomen of a little wood satyr butterfly, etc. If I could hear a magnification of the sounds of all insect mandibles dining on preys, it would eclipse the roar of the Niagara Falls. Nature's tableau is a forgery. Behind a facade of balance and harmonious serenity, a carnage of infinite ferocity, the rape and evisceration of millions of insects are being staged under the resplendent canopy of the green forest.

This macabre carnage strengthened my resolve. In Vedic mythology, anyone raising himself by knowledge upsets the comfort of heaven. The gods, ever watchful, live in terror of being outclassed. Did Jehovah behave any differently? Did he not spy on man because he feared him, because he saw him as a rival?

The sound of chimes from a babbling brook ended my reverie. My sneakers hit a protruding root, and I fell, bruising my head. Roots live in the darkness of the earth, inside the soil. Why had that tendril surfaced into that realm of light? Was it sick of living in the dark? I walked unsteadily on the green terrain.

He was naked, the old man with a patriarchal beard. His name was Cephissus, the river god. He begged for my forgiveness. He was making amends for the rape of Liriope, the wood nymph he had ravished. He had abandoned his son, Narcissus. He called me Narcissus. His evanescent form became fluid evaporating in the diaphanous air. Another hallucination, I pondered.

The ground was littered with decaying trunks from fallen trees. I reached the camping grounds and hid behind a pine tree. With binoculars, I scanned the scattered tents pitted on the grassy ground.

Alvard exited from his tent, a bottle in his hands. He collapsed on a folding chair, lit a cigar, and took a gulp from the bottle. After a while, he entered his tent, only to reappear with a mini telescope, a tripod, and a box attached to a metallic dish. Hauling these gadgets, he marched into the woods. I stalked him at a safe distance. One hundred and fifty feet was the distance a 9 mm bullet had to travel to do some damage. The Walther P38 had a range of ninety-eight meters or about three hundred feet. With my inadequate firing practice, I couldn't chance it. At a closer range, I'd make a kill. Then I'd trek back to my car and drive away with some certainty I'd have eliminated the threat.

My target set the tripod and adjusted the dish. With his telescope, he probed the foliage of the vast canopy. He turned on a switch, adjusted his earphones. Alvard was recording birdsongs. A particular tune emerged for the medley of forest sounds. It was shrill yet melodic. The bird was sabotaging my plans.

I didn't know Alvard was a weekend ornithologist. How could I silence an ornithologist?

Excess of deliberation frustrates all actions. Consciousness intervenes only to frustrate their execution. *"Consciousness is a perpetual interrogation of life; it is perhaps the ruin of life,"* Paul Valery wrote. It is an aberration to want to be different from what I am. One's survival is based on creating a fictitious self. I couldn't create the self of an assassin.

The recording of the birdsongs went on for more than an hour. He was enjoying himself. Then he collected his equipment and trekked back to the camping ground. I was still in my hiding place behind a venerable oak. I approached the birch tree, the residence for the singing bird. Throughout this intermission, its singing remained unchanged. I used the recording app on my cell phone to register its music. I was becoming an amateur ornithologist. Then I saw it. It had gray wings, a reddish neck, and a white belly. "The Songbirds of North America" had identified it in my cell phone. It was a robin.

On my trip back, I encountered a field of low-growing white flowers. The sweet scent of the plant elevated my mood. It was an ingredient of chamade: the lily of the valley. I uprooted a few stems.

The bouquet enchanted my wife. Her friend Eglantine was visiting her. She ran a neighborhood store which specialized in scented candles, exotic teas, and spices.

"Be careful you don't chew on them. It causes dizziness, fainting, and death."

"You don't say," I protested.

"Can't trust flowers, particularly those that look pure and holy," she voiced.

"So, what will happen if I make an infusion with these little white flowers?" I asked, intrigued.

"Lung failure," Eglantine warned.

"How could such a thing of beauty and fragrance be so deadly?" my wife protested.

"Plants protect themselves from predators by changing their chemistry to become killers," Eglantine voiced.

Oblivion

Only what we have not accomplished and what we couldn't accomplish matters to us. I should be proud of what I have not done. Such pride has to be invented. My liaison with Mantuo was threatened. An oyster to build up its shell must pass its weight in seawater through its body fifty thousand times. We hadn't built up a durable armor to protect us from the outside world. The shield was cracking, making us vulnerable. In Watteau's *Embarkation for Cythera*, couples in love are boarding a ship for the island of Cyprus, where Aphrodite was born. I'd elope with my mistress to the island of the lotus eaters, that land Ulysses visited where past and future are obliterated, that sanctuary where he forgot he had a father, a wife, and a son.

I was driving to the hospital immersed in a reverie of evasion when I received a call from Mantuo Luo. She wanted to visit the Bronx Botanical Garden. The Bronx's coat of arms has a motto in Latin: "No cede malis" (Yield to no evil).

That territory was named after Jonas Bronck, who settled the first Dutch settlement in the estuary of the Hudson River. I have always associated this borough with Edgar Allan Poe, who lived the last years of his life in a cottage now located on Kingsbridge Road.

We wandered gravel paths shadowed by trees with nameplates identifying their genealogy. She approached a flowering bush: aconitum. The flowers were blue cylindrical hoods.

"We call it Fu Zi. Zhang Zhongjing says it makes the dead come back," she announced.

Willows, acacias, baobabs and banyans, cinnamon trees and sycamores, magnolias and eucalyptus garnished the grounds of the arboretum. The air was scented with sap, resin, and chlorophyll.

She approached a tree with exquisite white flowers: cerbera odollam.

"Hai manguo," she announced.

A herbal encyclopedia in my phone nicknamed it "the suicide tree in India." If you stood beneath its branches, the rain passing through the leaves and absorbing all the toxins would then fall on your skin disfiguring it and entering your bloodstream through your pores, will precipitate cardiac arrest. It contains a potent toxin cerberin which blocks ion channels in heart muscles. There was no label warning park visitors to avoid contact with this lethal plant. I planned to call the botanical garden's director and alert him.

Mantuo drew near the trumpetlike flowers dangling from the branches of a large bush. She stared at it, trancelike. Was there was a bond between them, cross-species connectivity?

"I'm very thirsty," she whispered.

We walked to the cafeteria.

We ordered fruit juices. She excused herself. I checked my messages. Hospital stuff.

Then a message from Alvard: "*Soyez prudent!*"

Was it a warning, a trick to derail his adversary? Was he alerting me of his design to hurt me? Was it the start of a campaign of harassment?

Mantuo Luo returned. Bewitchingly, she had adorned her face with white powder and delineated her eyes with a turquoise mascara. I studied her painted face, searching for clues. The makeup had drowned any signs her facial lines could reveal. She was inward, visiting some secret space, involved in some internal dialogue with an invisible conversationalist.

"Would you like to visit the greenhouse?" I asked.

"I want to go home."

WQXR, the classical music station, was playing "Death and Transfiguration" by Richard Strauss. What was the significance of that tree? She had exhibited affection and tenderness for its white flowers. She hadn't identified it or named it in Mandarin.

A fatal accident in the Long Island Expressway last night, causing a one-hour traffic delay, was reported. A man crashed his Range

Rover against a milk tanker. The driver was trapped in his car. The firemen sliced through the steel to retrieve his mangled body.

"Alvard came to see me," she said.

"When?" I asked, alarmed.

"Last night."

"What did he want?"

"He wanted massage," she said.

"Did you fuck him?"

She didn't answer.

"I should have taken care of this problem long time ago. I am sorry."

"It's the last time."

"He will not go away, Mantuo."

"He will never touch me again."

She embraced me. I was beyond repair.

I drove Mantuo Luo home. She wanted me to come up. I declined. I wanted to be alone, preferring the vanishing.

My Mother Leaves Me

I received a phone call from the police. My mother died. Her neighbor and friend had found her at the bottom of the staircase. She had fallen. I was surprised by the cause of death. My mother had joined a gym and was a frequent visitor. She had been taking Pilates classes for many years. The friend had contacted the funeral home. Her body was preserved there.

I wondered if my visit had quickened memory, stirred latent embers.

This event had little impact. I don't subscribe to the theory that the loss of parents always transforms us and that we become adults. We never become completely adults.

I refused to see her corpse. I've seen a lot of corpses. That's a corpse I didn't want my retina to encounter. That image would become imprinted for eternity. I want to remember her drinking mint and cinnamon tea.

I called the funeral home and spoke to a mortician. He was Sicilian. His voice was sunny and comforting. I told him to take care of everything, to recommend a cemetery. I didn't want her cremated. I wanted her body to be embraced in a white shroud, no coffin, and to be buried like Jews and Moslems do to facilitate the decomposition of the corpse, allowing the minerals to be returned to the earth she loved. A compost. I didn't want a funeral. I was specific about my demands. He agreed to all my requests.

I had some explaining to do. I'll justify my decisions to my wife and daughter to exclude them from this ritual. Who wants to look at a dead parent? I reread *The Stranger* by Albert Camus. The main character, Meursault, hadn't visited his mother in the nursing home for months.

DAVID DORIAN

And then she died. Who could forget the first sentence of that novel? My mother died yesterday, or was it the day before yesterday? It says it all. But his guilt for neglecting his mother finally gets him. I'm not experiencing any guilt.

Blood Rites

I crossed the Williamsburg Bridge and veered off to Mulberry Street. These days I've been expecting a visit from the Furies. Why haven't they exacted their pounds of flesh? Why haven't they driven me to madness like when they haunted Orestes after he stabbed his mother? Enfeebled by conscience, I will offer meager resistance to their rapacious teeth.

I walked the narrow pavements. In the seedy carnival ambience of Mott Street, I ambled colliding against insomniacs. Strident Chinese string music mixed with the lamenting notes of Sicilian ballads. Outside a Szechuan restaurant, Chinese hostesses in flowing gowns were entreating tourists to savor the culinary delicacies of their region. Under a cherry-red-and-green awning, a maître d'hôtel was flaunting the Neapolitan plat du jour to a group of traveling elderly women. Scents of Italian sauces collided with the aroma of steamed pork dumplings. I wandered through the maze of narrow streets lit by flickering neon signs advertising noodle houses.

A Catholic church at the end of the street beckoned. On the brick facade, a slabstone read:

Franciscan Fathers
Church of the
Most Precious Blood

As a surgeon, I had an intimate relationship with blood. When I'd visited the bowels of a patient, my gloved fingers bathed in that vermillion liquid. I stood in front of that church contemplating its brick facade. Two stone angels held amphora full of the Savior's blood. Medicine and Christianity have a lot in common. A church is a hospital for the soul. As a patient, I needed a transfusion because I had lost lots of blood. I need to check in that spiritual clinic and commence treatment, I thought.

I knocked on the main door. It was locked. I walked into the side alley and found a door.

"The church is closed," the old man said.

"How can you close a church?"

"For renovation! A water pipe broke," he said.

"A church gotta be open 24-7 like the emergency room in a hospital."

Inside the church, the nave was painted white. Stained glass windows reflected the flames of an army of candles. It reminded me of a Rococo Church I had visited in Venice on my honeymoon. Two large crucifixes towered over the rows of pews.

"How can I help you?"

"Can we speak in your office?"

"This is my office."

He sat in a pew and invited me to join him. He lit a cigarette. It was a Lucky Strike.

"That's the brand that won the war," I said.

"It ain't over yet."

He paused.

"I'm not a Catholic. I don't believe in God. Is that a problem?"

"Is that a problem?" the priest repeated.

"I want to kill a man, a friend."

"The war isn't over," he repeated.

"He used to be a friend?"

"Why didn't you do it already?" he asked.

I wasn't ready for that interrogation.

"He records birdsongs," I said.

"Our patron Saint Francis preached to the birds. He'd talk to them."

He paused and became reflective.

"Birds can be nasty. Have you heard about the honeyguide bird?" he asked.

"No."

"It's an African bird as big as a New York sparrow with gray and brown feathers. Nothing to look at. It eats wild honey but can't get to the beehive inside the trunk of trees because of the bees, so it looks for an animal with a big fur coat that likes honey and guides them to the beehive. The animal gets the hive from the tree and feasts on the honey. Then it's his turn. He goes after the leftovers. That's the good part of the story. Now the not-so-good part of the story. Every honeyguide baby bird is born with a hook at the corner of its beak. Its function is to cut the throat of its baby brothers or sisters. And once it has murdered its brethren, the hook falls. It doesn't need it anymore."

"Mean bird!"

"Evil exists. That's why we gotta fight back. You didn't kill your friend and now you want another chance?"

"I don't know."

"It's about a woman," he announced.

"Yes."

"You know, two of the first books, the Iliad and the Ramayana, are about men who stole women who were not theirs. Men have been killing each other for thousands of years because of women. The way of all flesh. But there are some men…"

"What do you mean?"

"You love her! Or you think you love her. That sin got a name: idolatry, we call it, the veneration of idols, of false gods."

"Father, I was never baptized. Would you baptize me?"

"Why would I do that?"

"My soul needs a shower."

He directed me to the fount of holy water and sprinkled some drops on my forehead. He said some words in Latin.

"What's next?" I asked.

"Be grateful to that singing bird."

"I should be grateful?"

"Yes, indebted."

"Birds are everywhere in all the holy texts: the dove for the Christians, the owl for Athena, the simurgh for the Persians, the eagle for Odin, etc."

He walked away, quietly.

Inside the church, I felt attracted by all the burning candles. Molten wax was oozing, spilling into an immense marble counter. I lit a candle.

Chords from the organ reverberated in the vast nave. The priest was playing Bach's *Saint Matthew's Passion*. I knew that piece well in my student days when I took a class on Baroque music. I went on my knees at the feet of the porcelain body of Christ nailed against a wall.

I thought of *Madame Butterfly*, a Japanese woman from the nobility who falls in love with an American naval officer who impregnates her and abandons her. She gives birth to the child and commits hara-kiri. In "Turandot," a Chinese princess who shuns men is forced for political reasons to marry. She proposes a test to be taken by contenders. If they fail to solve the riddle, they are beheaded the next dawn. Many candidates lose their life. She's a killer, merciless and unforgiving. Two Asian women with two different attitudes on love.

I walked out of the church.

Gentians

I walked down Eldridge Street and found a café with wicker chairs in the veranda. I ordered a double espresso. I felt depleted, like after a great squandering of energy. Sparrows flew from the nearby tree and aggregated around my chair. They were accustomed to tourists. I asked the waiter to bring me bread to feed my flock. I threw crumbs at the rapacious beaks. They assaulted each other. I dropped my last morsel and watched the big ones bully the small ones. These creatures were earthbound. Their wings wouldn't lift them beyond few feet from the ground. They, too, belong to the earth. I recalled a science teacher in high school who told us that nothing of what exists on earth can ever leave. We are all in bondage, shackled to a slave galley.

A dirty little barefoot girl came padding up to me, proffering blue flowers. I bought the whole bouquet and handed her loose bills. She grabbed my money and darted. I wanted to hear her hard-luck story, to adopt her for a few minutes. I thought of my daughter.

I reached the sanctuary of my car and entered its consoling space. I downloaded the horoscope app and stated my birthday. "Your quote for the day," the woman's voice reverberated. "*Recall the here for the sake of the hereafter.*"

I drove home, fighting the fatigue that was creeping on me. I arrived at the first rays. My wife wasn't home. She'd gone to her yoga retreat. I filled the vase with tap water, which had a strong smell of rust from the miles and miles of decaying pipes. I placed the flowers on the mahogany table and sat on the armchair to contemplate them. They were gentians, the flowers I had taken to the cemetery to my father's grave. The Ancient Greeks believed they glowed in the darkness of the corridors of Hades lightning the path for the traveler.

*****

The next morning on my drive to the hospital, I turned on the news. There was an updated report about the accident the car radio had aired last night. The driver of the Range Rover was swerving erratically when he collided against the truck. He was identified as a doctor at Good Samaritan Hospital.

I called the hospital. The receptionist was distraught.

"Did you hear the news?" she asked, grieving.

"What happened?"

"Dr. Norst," she panted.

"When?"

"Last night!"

He had visited Mantuo Luo last night, and he was returning to his apartment in the Upper West Side. I suddenly felt I was inside a vacuum. My lungs were pumping in an airless planet. Using a few molecules of oxygen I had stored in some random alveoli, I maintained feeble control of my brain. I maneuvered to the shoulder of the highway and turned off the engine. My trachea was closing fast, and I didn't have my inhaler with me. I had stopped carrying it for months because I hadn't needed it. I crawled to the back seat.

The news of Alvard's death at a time when I'd wished his death was a traumatic event. The asthma attack was a retaliation for my murderous yearning, I thought. Based on the archaic law of talion, my superego was sentencing me. I was a witness to my own execution: death by strangulation, by suffocation, by drowning like the character from the story "The Judgment" by Kafka, a son who wished his father harm. No air was entering my lungs, and my alveoli were screaming. I felt that same nausea when, refusing to chew coca leaves to alleviate the scarcity of oxygen, I naively went on a climb to Machu Picchu. A drowning man grasping floating driftwood. I was flaying. My right hand groped inside the pocket situated at the back of the passenger seat. I felt the metal cylinder. I had forgotten that in my days of frequent asthma attacks, I stashed extra inhalers everywhere. I ripped the seal off with my teeth and pressed the button. Albuterol poured into my constricted bronchi. Oxygen flushed all the capillaries of my lungs. I was inhaling loudly, saturating my lungs, replenishing all the cells.

Restored, I started the engine and drove to the city.

As soon as I came in the Department of Surgery, Olga, the head nurse, rushed in. Grief and consternation wrinkled her face. Doctors in the hospital were frazzled by the death of their colleague. The staff was silent, mourning the loss of one of their own. I sequestered myself in my office and locked the door. I grabbed the bottle of bourbon from the bottom drawer and filled the paper cup.

The accident of last night was amply featured in the news website. His battered Rover mobilized many firemen cutting through the metal. The driver of the milk truck, who survived, had driven from Michigan nonstop. Fatigue was blamed for the accident. There was another theory a news analyst promulgated. Ten percent of automobile fatalities remain unexplained: no bad weather, no mechanical failure, no driver's fatigue, no excessive speed, no cell phone distractions. He believed insects are the culprits. A wasp, a bee, a spider, or a moth trapped inside a car can cause havoc in the highway where drivers exceed state limits. The driver goes into panic, tries to swat the bug, or unrolls the window to let it out. He loses control of his vehicle. Inside the car, an accident scene investigator found a dead hornet. Repeatedly, I called Mantuo Luo. She was not answering. I called my wife and told her the news. I rang Mantuo Luo again.

A sense of irresolution was nagging. I opened my laptop and visited the website of the Bronx Botanical Garden. A function on that page allowed the viewer to look at photos of the trees in the garden. I recognized that tree with the long droopy flowers with the off-white corolla with whom Mantuo Luo had a moment of silent intimacy. *Datura stramonium* was its Latin name, a member of the nightshade family, like potato, tomato, tobacco, and henbane. It is full of energy and aggression. It has a huge defense system, a chemical arsenal to protect itself against its enemies. It's full of tropane alkaloids, scopolamine, hyoscyamine, atropine, and many others. If ingested, it can cause photophobia, delirium, mania, a complete inability to differentiate reality from fantasy, tachycardia, and other ailments. It was used in ancient Chinese medicine as a powerful analgesic by the discoverer of anesthesia, Hua Tuo, who prescribed it before surgery. He recommended it as an effective treatment for asthma. Mantuo applied massage oil on my skin. In my research on the toxicity of certain plants, I found that the Ancient Greeks had one word, which translated both as medicine and poison. It was the word *pharmakon* which has given our word *pharmacy*. The difference between medicine and poison, according to the Greek physician Diocorides, is in the dosage. A small amount has healing properties; a large dosage is fatal. I presume Mantuo Luo was giving me a calculated measure of datura oil mixed in her massage ointment to treat my asthma, a dosage that was therapeutic. She was her father's daughter, the heiress of his herbal trove. He taught her about Datura, the flower from heaven and hell. She could have ended my life every time she anointed my body with her hypnotic elixir. Instead she cured my asthma, a chronic ailment that could have shortened my life. I was now sure of her love. She had cured Alvard of his skin condition when several dermatologists had failed. She was a witch doctor versed in the arcane wisdom of botanical medicine, a tradition her people had practiced for millennia. On her last encounter with Alvard, did she spike the massage oil with a large dose of Datura essences? Did the extracts infiltrate his permeable skin through a million pores gushing into his arteries, which carried its stupefying ingredients to his brain, causing havoc among the neurotransmitters, leading to disorientation and collision in the highway? Hadrian Virgilius, the owner of that jazz club *Jezebel's* where Alvard was often performing, met Mantuo Luo at an AA meeting. He was in a car accident on his trip to his beach bungalow in Maine. Shien Lieu, the Chinese rehabilitation camp commandant who had abused Mantuo Luo, fell from the thirty-third floor of that government building. She had given the Chinese name of all trees in the museum arboretum except Datura. The name of her bunk bed mate, the girl with a limp, was Ju, Chrysanthemum. I asked Mantuo Luo what the meaning of her name was, and she told me it was a white flower. Also, the kimono in her massage room was decorated with embroidered bell-like white flowers. I accessed the foreign language translator app, typed *Datura stramonium*, and pressed Enter. A few seconds later, the name appeared: Mantuo Luo.

I drove to Montefiore Hospital in the Bronx to meet Dr. Lawrence Garrick, a toxicologist. He brewed coffee he brought from Mexico. The coffee box showed a photograph of El Castillo, the main pyramid in Chichen Itza.

"Those Mayans, they were master herbalists and toxicologists?" he claimed.

"I'd like to know about Datura?" I asked.

"Ah, the goddess. Toloache in Mayan. Gorgeous flowers, decadent, luxuriant, opulent. Demonic! Do you know if you have a datura bush in your bedroom, you will inhale her scent and hallucinate? It gets its energy at night. Deadly!"

"Could you tell me more?"

"It's also called Thorn Apple, Jimson Weed. In Mozambique, the Tsongas use it in girls' initiation ceremonies and for exorcism. The Chumashin of Central California drink a decoction for prophetic dreams. They call it 'dream helper.' In India, the cult of Kali worshippers called Thugges used Datura to stupefy their victims before strangling them. The British stamped out the cult in 1830, and Sir William Sleeman arrested three thousand Thuggees and executed four hundred of them. God Shiva, the god of Yogis, carried a Datura. The great herbalist Daniel Schulke had the perfect name for this diabolical plant: chronophagoi, 'time eaters.'"

"I am afraid a friend of mine has been using it."

"Has he suffered from episodes of vertigo?"

"Yes."

"Nausea?"

"Yes."

"Hallucinations, visual and/or auditory, olfactory?"

"Yes."

"Datura breaks the walls between what's real and what's unreal. You know, this cursed plant blurs the boundaries."

"I didn't know."

"The toxins in the pollen, the leaves, the seeds. and mostly the roots get deposited in the body. They concentrate in the tissues. and they are not excreted. After a while, every organ shuts down."

"How does it affect mental functioning?"

"Well, memory gets progressively lost. For the organs too. The heart will forget to beat. The liver just won't hear the message from the medulla oblongata to produce more liver enzymes."

"You talked about hallucinations?"

"Yes, you'd talk to people who are not there, I mean physically, or smell some fragrance that's not in the air. Would you like more coffee?"

"Please."

"You know the Aztecs used to feed that plant to prisoners they were going to sacrifice, they'd give them Datura seeds, which made them docile because they were hallucinating. Then they made them climb the steps of the pyramid and pull out their hearts."

"Yes I read about Aztec sacrifices. I didn't know they sedated their victims."

"Why are you wearing sunglasses in winter?" he asked, pointing at them in my shirt pocket.

"I've become sensitive to light," I replied.

He stopped talking and became silent.

"Photosensitivity is a symptom. You're a doctor, for heaven's sake. How could you be so reckless?" he blew up.

"It's in the massage oil. This Chinese masseuse I've been going to for months."

"She's Chinese you say?"

"Yes, her father was an herbalist in Tien Jin."

"It's in the dosage, in the dosage. It was an ingredient in ancient Chinese medicine, but tiny amounts. But the symptoms you're suffering from are evidence of substantial doses."

"She's cured my asthma."

"And poisoned you!"

"I got to know her name and place of business."

"I'll tell you all I know."

"We have to call the police. Did she work in a salon?"

"Yes."
"Was she referred to you?"
"Yes, by a colleague."
"I want to speak with him."
"Why?"
"He was probably poisoned too."
"You can't. He was killed in a vehicular accident, last week."
"What happened?"
"The police report says it's a truck driver's fault. He had been driving for eleven hours. Fatigue is to blame, they say."
"In all probability, lost control of the car because he was hallucinating. What was her name?"
"Mantuo Luo."
"My god! That's Chinese for Datura. You don't know her real name, do you?"

Dr. Garrick collapsed on his chair, his eyes staring at some distant landscape. He woke up from his trance, rubbing his face vigorously.

"I have a question to ask you, the most important question of all, the ultimate question: are you hallucinating now?"

I left his office shaken. The questions kept kicking the gate of my consciousness. I remember the potted plant with white flowers I had offered my mother. I had placed it in her bedroom, by the window. At night that flower sprays pollen. My mother had been breathing it for month. She fell down the stairs. That's how she died. She lost balance because the poison was messing up her gyroscope. Who was Mantuo? Calypso or Circe? Did she kill all her lovers? Why this murderous rage? I was primed to be her last victim, but somehow I was spared. My photosensitivity, bouts of dizziness, hallucinations are the results of her slow poisoning. Why did I start an affair with this woman? No live organism can continue for long to exist sanely under conditions of absolute reality. She offered me an alternate world. The essences in the ointments messed me up. I acted out what I had repressed for so long.

I don't want to go to the police. I want to deliver the justice that is due. I want to be the punisher. I don't want to frighten her.

She'll run away and vanish. Or she'll flee to her home country. I'll check myself in a psychiatric hospital they will commit me and keep me there. I will be safe, and she'll come to visit me one day. I cannot write anymore. I am losing words. My head hurts terribly. I'm so tired I can't drive in the state I'm in. There's a broken switch somewhere or a circuit breaker that doesn't work anymore. I'm calling the psychiatric hospital to send an ambulance: SOS!

In the hospital room, things are reduced to a minimum. I no longer have any desire to understand the world. I watch TV for hours. It numbs the last sensations. When you give up on life, the last remaining contacts are those you need to prolong your days: doctors, nurses, health providers, etc. I think of my wife, one of those souls who are capable of devoting their lives to someone's happiness. But throughout her days, she never saved a life, while I saved hundreds. She saved mine. She created our daughter, her gift to me. But our children come from us but are separate from us. They chart their existence with coordinates of their own making. I will die soon. My burial would be simple. I'd read that Thai people don't believe in ghosts and have little interest in the fate of the body after death; that's why many are buried in mass graves.

Epilogue

There was no more entry into the diary. Maren's thoughts whirled, collided, exploding like clashing asteroids. She felt her pulse throbbing, blood streaming down her arms, bursting through the tiny veins in her face, flooding her brain. A shard of guilt lacerated her. She had been oblivious to his progressive disintegration. It took five years to reach the abyss. Signs and vestiges of trickery she missed. In her naivete, she had been an enabler, collaborating in her silence to his imminent downfall.

Gabriel had divulged everything. Maren remembered a dinner with Alvard and Farhana where Alvard told about a patient treated by Jung, a patient with a physical illness that was relieved by confession, how the mind can heal the body. Is Gabriel's confession a forward step in his treatment, a strong willingness to get better?

Her husband had been unfaithful, shattered the idols of the hearth. He had entertained a complex and profound relationship with the Asian woman. This liaison transcended the traditional norms of an illicit affair. He had been lured and infected by a potent deliriant administered cutaneously. Gabriel D'Arcy was reading *The Botany of Desire*. It was a love affair, with a woman, with a plant. That flowery plant in his room, it was *Datura stramonium*, which produces nocturnal exhalations Gabriel inhales every night in his sleep. His addiction was unabated. He was in a perpetual state of hallucinations brought about by the psychotropic chemicals inherent in *Datura stramonium*.

Maren was no alkaloid apparition. She was muscle and bone with a heart that gushed with unadulterated life. She'd fight for her husband; she'd break the trance. She'd abduct him from that soporific hell, the lair of Mantuo Luo and that cursed flower, a female Orpheus rescuing Euridice from the Underworld, hauling him to the world of the living, like Demeter resurrecting her daughter, Persephone, from Hades.

Maren was fired up by the anticipation of the war she was about to wage. She executed a sharp U-turn and drove back to the sanatorium. She'll reveal Gabriel's diary to the director of the Department of Neuropharmacology; she'll haul away the Datura plant from his room and demand a cleansing of all the toxins stored in his organs. It'd be a salvage operation of a soul about to exit the plane of the living. That diary Alvard wrote sleeps inside the hard drive of a laptop somewhere. She'll locate that computer and extract its content. And more will be revealed. Strategies will be used. She will intercede with that hidden god only atheists pray to. She heard herself mutter: "Lord, may it become for us an everlasting healing…" And if that stone-deaf and tongue-tied Almighty doesn't answer, she, a negligible mortal, will shatter the harmony of heaven and she will stalk that Medusa in her Asian lair and witness her cremation.

About the Author

Immersed in the radiant culture of Europe, David Dorian writes novels for the American reader he cherishes. Educated in a white city in the Mediterranean and in Paris, he followed his emotional compass and landed in the New World. Transplanted in New York City, he absorbed the artistic nutrients the city offered. He gave in return to his adopted city and enriched us with his vibrant luminous sensibility. He taught comparative literature and philosophy. His lectures on Baudelaire, Gerard de Nerval, Rimbaud, and Mallarme attracted many avid souls. Flaubert and Zola he lionized. He became a hypnotherapist and altered spirits in distress. As a psychoanalyst, he investigated souls in peril and healed many marooned hearts. His yearning for esthetics and sensuality in a world that is becoming more artificial and virtual is restorative and empowering. In his novels, the human characters experience reality with all their senses. They interact with each other with ebullience and exhilaration. They feel with fervor and explore their environment with savage intensity. Always attracted by the other side of the moon, this author delves into the deep end of the heart and encounters fantasmagorie entities. He exposes the ghostly shadows that slither beneath the surface. As a psychologist, he has encountered that ravenous bestiary inside souls, that menagerie that wants to break the shackles and go on a rampage. In his novels, his characters are embattled. They are cursed, damned, and their struggle to reach the light is epic. Read him and be haunted.

CPSIA information can be obtained
at www.ICGtesting.com
Printed in the USA
FSHW021644250620
71391FS